HONEY'S WEREWOLF

Big City Lycans
Book Three

New York Times and USA Today Bestselling Author

Eve Langlais

Copyright Honey's Werewolf © Eve Langlais 2022/2023

Cover Art © by Melony Paradise of ParadiseCoverDesign.com 2022

Produced in Canada

Published by Eve Langlais

http://www.EveLanglais.com

eBook: ISBN: 978 1 77 384 3605

Print ISBN: 978 1 77 384 3612

ALL RIGHTS RESERVED

This book is a work of fiction and the characters, events and dialogue found within the story are of the author's imagination and are not to be construed as real. Any resemblance to actual events or persons, either living or deceased, is completely coincidental.

No part of this book may be reproduced or shared in any form or by any means, electronic or mechanical, including but not limited to digital copying, file sharing, audio recording, email and printing without permission in writing from the author.

1

Losing her just about killed him. Ulric's apartment just wasn't the same. His bed felt so empty. His days unfulfilled since her departure. No more meaning left.

He'd not had much of a choice. He had to let her go. Brandy—a good friend of his and the owner of Princess Froufrou—had returned home and expected her cat back.

The horror. Ulric had gotten quite close to the regal feline. She kept him on his toes with her demands. Took so much from him—including a few pints of blood—but when she allowed him to pet her sleek fur, and even better purred, it was worth it.

What would he do without his precious queen?

With work done for the day, he sauntered slowly back to his empty apartment. There would be no need to de-lint his pillow, couch, or the black jeans he'd kept hiding and finding covered in hair. There would be no impatient meowing as he opened a can of food, no need for a bandage for the scratch because he fed her too slowly.

Such sadness. Maybe he should pay Brandy a visit. See if Princess Froufrou still even remembered him.

As he passed a storefront—Muddy Mutts Pet Supplies and Grooming—his gaze snagged on an oversized cage inside. As if drawn by some special force, he opened the door, an oversized boy entering a pet shop for the very first time.

As a Lycan, who went furry on the full moon, it felt shameful to be in such a place. A wolf didn't have need of anti-dandruff shampoo, flea and tick treatment, or a muzzle. He almost turned and ran. And then he saw it.

A teeny, tiny furball sitting at the bars of the cage, staring at him.

He stared right back. His heart stopped.

The striped kitten, barely the size of his fist, yawned and laid down. Lonely and dejected in its prison.

I'll save you!

A sign zip tied to the cage caught his attention. *Kittens for sale*. With the s crossed out. Only one left. If fate had a feeling, it hit him then and there.

He approached the bars and looked at it closer. It pretended to sleep. Probably not wanting to get its hopes up.

He lifted a hand as someone cleared their throat. "Please don't put your fingers in the cage."

"Why?" he asked, turning his head as the tip of a digit poked through the bars into fur.

Tiny needles pierced the end of his finger. His mouth rounded as the kitten chomped while growling.

"That's why," was the dry reply. "It's not very friendly."

"Can you blame the little thing? It's locked in a prison."

"Buy it and you can set it free," was the sarcastic drawl from the woman.

"How much?" he asked. Which led to some negotiating, a list of required items, and a dent on his credit card of more than twelve hundred dollars. He also needed to call Dorian for a ride back to his place since he couldn't carry everything by himself.

"Why would you buy a cat?" Dorian asked, eyeing Ulric in the passenger seat of his car, a very posh and expensive travel carrier on his lap.

The little kitten didn't appear impressed at being locked away again, but as Jenny—according to her name tag—had claimed, without one he'd lose the cat before he went a block. Knowing Brandy did the same for Princess Froufrou, he agreed.

But the kitten wanted blood.

"Finding this cat was fate," Ulric replied to his friend. He then leaned close to one of the mesh windows on the carrier to whisper, "Soon we'll be home and I'll feed you all kinds of yummy stuff."

Claws managed to explode from the tiny holes and almost caught his lip.

"You know, I realized you were lonely, but a cat, of all things..." Dorian shook his head. "Does this mean you're going to become the cat man?"

"I read that it's good to have pets as you get older. You should think of getting something."

Dorian snorted. "Unlike you, I'm not lonely."

"Because you're always on your computer. Virtual reality isn't the same as in-person contact."

"Says you. I find it works great for me. So does the kitten mean you've given up on your quest to find the perfect lady?"

"Nope. I have lots of love to give." Now if only he could find someone to give it to!

"I'm assuming it's a girl given all your shit is pink."

"Yup. I'm going to call her Queen Fuzzbottom."

That had Dorian choking. "You're kidding, right?"

"Queen Fluff?"

"Why not wait a few days, get to know the creature, and then figure it out based on its personality? Given its antics thus far, I'm gonna throw Savage into the ring."

"More like Feisty," Ulric crooned as the bag rocked on his lap.

The moment he got home and let the kitten loose it bolted. And Ulric chased. The cat went under the couch, 'round the table in the kitchen, whipped up the curtain left behind by the previous tenants, jumped to the top of a bookcase, and then put itself in pounce position, hissing.

Ulric could have snagged it, but he remembered what it took to tame Princess Froufrou when she got in a mood.

"Is the baby hungry?" he murmured as he unpacked his many purchases, the cans of wet food being his goal.

The carved wooden dish went on a feeding mat on the floor. He cracked open the can, and as he bent down to dump it, something small with sharp claws landed on his back and used him to climb down to the floor. The kitten went at it aggressively, obviously starving. A good thing he'd saved her from the store!

He went to stroke her, only to leave his hand hovering as she whipped her head around and growled, showing some teeth.

Maybe he'd wait until she was done.

As she chewed, he set up the kitty litter box. He had experience with the noxiousness that happened in it. But he didn't hold it against Princess Froufrou, given he did worse sometimes in his own bathroom.

He'd bought a covered model with the most odor-trapping granules and a carpet to catch stray gravel. Jenny had mentioned he could order a robotic version that actually removed the poop and pee for him, but he'd be shelling out another grand for it.

The setup was finished just in time as his satisfied kitten sauntered over, belly swaying. It hopped into the box and proceeded to create the most awful smell, followed by vigorous kicking and digging in the litter. Sand flew out the opening, shooting over the carpet to hit his parquet floor, skittering as it spread.

When the kitten came out, she stood and eyed him. Meowed.

"What is it, Princess Fluff?"

The instant hiss let him know he'd said the wrong thing.

"You don't like that name?" He crouched down far enough his long beard dangled in front of the cat.

Instant pounce. The kitten threw itself wholeheartedly at destroying his beard. It dug its claws in, bit and chewed at the hair.

It made him so happy. He'd not realized how lonely he'd been until he babysat the demanding Princess Froufrou. Having a purpose, even if caring for someone else, eased the lonely ache inside. Was it any wonder he'd bought the kitten who'd climbed to perch atop his head, biting and digging in claws, ensuring compliance from his obviously evil scalp?

Despite Dorian's teasing, Ulric understood a pet wasn't a replacement for love. He'd seen his friends who succumbed: Griffin with his many smiles, Wendell who'd reconnected with his old flame Bernard, even the dour Billy finally looked relaxed since hooking up with Brandy. Lucky bastards. Ulric kept looking for Mrs. Right. Dated all kinds of woman looking for *the one*.

Alas, the only female pussy interested in him weighed a few pounds and had chosen to return to his beard and got caught. Like seriously tangled. Paws, claws, poor thing appeared trapped. Not that she panicked. The kitten went to sleep; however, Ulric went bolting for help.

Given he didn't want to deal with the amusement of his pack brothers or hurt his little princess trying to extricate her on his own, he chose to visit the new vet office down the block, open until eight on Thursdays, which was lucky for him.

Less ideal?

The absolutely gorgeous woman who took one look at him and laughed.

Ulric usually would have joined in, but staring at Dr. Iris, it hit him like a lightning bolt.

I've found her. The one.

And just his luck, she wore a wedding ring.

2

Honey's receptionist tried to warn her. Francis had drawn her aside to whisper, "He's got a cat stuck in his beard."

Still, knowing and seeing it? Two different things.

Entering the examination room at the veterinary clinic—hers if you didn't count hefty payments given each month to the bank—Honey did her best to not giggle. And failed.

She couldn't help laughing at the sight of the veritable Viking with the kitten having a tangled nap in his impressive beard. The chin growth was blond like the hair on his head but, with dark brows, striking to say the least. And big. Not fat big, but tall and wide, his shoulders broad enough to make even Honey feel petite. Not something that happened often.

A tall girl herself at over six feet, Honey had a difficult time finding partners not intimidated by her size.

While she would date a man of any height so long as he wasn't a douche, she ran into issues with men both taller and shorter. *You're just not dainty,* said by Jerome of six foot four. *I hate that you can reach the high shelves without a chair,* complained Hugh of five foot ten.

Only one man ever looked at her and truly celebrated her height. Unfortunately, her dear Rocko died young.

But now she'd found another to eyeball her with interest. His gaze unabashedly roved her head to toe until he spotted the ring on her finger. Then he appeared stricken.

She could have explained she was a widow. However, she made it a point to never date clients, hence why she still wore the ring to work.

He recovered from his brief disappointment and flashed her a big smile. "Doctor, so glad you were able to see me on such short notice."

"My receptionist said you sounded quite frantic, and I can see why. May I?" She indicated his beard.

"You won't hurt my kitty, right?"

"I'm going to pretend you didn't say that given my profession is to help animals."

He apologized immediately. "I'm sorry, Doctor, I'm just worried. As you can see, she is very tiny and fragile."

"And apparently likes you very much." Honey wasn't surprised to see such a masculine example with a tiny pet. Love was love. Although she would admit to finding it vastly entertaining that those kinds of pairings were most likely to have an overly doting owner.

"Together less than a day and already we formed a bond." He beamed somewhat sappishly, but it didn't detract from his good looks.

She poked at his beard, the long, wiry hair softer than expected. Strong too. Slight tugs didn't break it.

He stopped breathing as she stroked the kitten who slept on but began to purr, a little engine of content.

She withdrew her hand. "Do you want the good news or the bad news?"

"Hit me with the bad." He closed his eyes and braced.

Rather than giggle again, she bit her inner cheek and said, "The bad news is we'll have to trim off your beard."

"By trim, you're talking one inch, two?" He sounded hopeful. Perhaps he planned an audition for that show with those long-bearded guys in camo, *Duck Dynasty*, or was she thinking of the motorcycle one?

"Given how high your cat is tucked, and if we want some slack to work with, it's best if we trim close to the jaw."

"Can't we untangle her so we can save the beard?"

"Remember how you told me she is fragile?"

He sighed. "Fine then. If you must. And here I'd almost broken a record in managing to keep it more than six months."

She blinked at him. "You grow hair that fast?"

He flashed those pearly whites again. "It runs in my family."

She shook her head. "Must be nice. My dad is completely bald and has been since I was little."

"My condolences," he offered somberly.

She shook her head and bit back a smile. He really was entertaining. "I'll need you to lean down so your beard and most of the kitten's weight is resting on the table." She indicated as she snared scissors from a drawer.

He bent over, draping his heavy beard on the steel surface, and joked, "I feel like I'm readying for the guillotine."

She snipped her scissors. "Well, you are losing a part of you."

His chuckle made her tingle head to toe. She ignored it as she leaned close enough to mutter, "Hold still." She clipped carefully close to his jaw, loosening the strands in the front. When she'd cut them through, he angled his chin up, exposing the ones farther back.

When the last section separated, he rose and rubbed his ragged chin. "Feels so light." He eyed the discarded hairball with the smaller furball inside. "Now where will she snuggle?"

"Fear not, she will inconvenience another part of your body. It's what cats do."

Allergic? Guaranteed the antisocial cat would

insist on lap sitting. Wanted to sleep? Would use your head as its mattress.

"I hope so. She's my first. I don't want to mess anything up."

"You'll be fine. Cats have a way of letting you know their needs." Sometimes with sharp teeth to a nose if you missed their feeding time by thirty seconds. Honey loved animals, but Mom's cat, Precious, was a demon. "Now shall we extricate your feline?"

Honey aimed her scissors, only to pause as the kitten stirred in the nest of hair, stretching and squirming. Then it emerged from the hairball with utter ease.

She blinked. Waited for the giant to say something. Like lose his shit because, apparently, they'd cut his beard for nothing. Trust a cat to make her look bad.

He didn't appear angry at all but rather amused. "What a brat. Sorry I wasted your time, but, hey, since you're already here, I don't suppose you'd give my new baby an exam. The store I adopted her from say she's healthy and all that but doesn't hurt to be sure."

"Did this store mention the age or give you any paperwork?"

He dug into his jacket and pulled out his phone, flicking it before turning to show the screen. "This is the email I was sent with my receipt and stuff."

According to his email, the kitten was fourteen weeks old. Due for its second set of shots but had its first. Was one of seven in the litter and... Oh. She absorbed the next interesting tidbit as she scrolled the rest of the email, including the amount he'd paid not just for overpriced stuff but the cat itself.

"You shelled out five hundred dollars for a cat with only a single set of shots?" That was a rip-off for what amounted to a basic domestic breed.

"I know, it was a steal considering the cuteness. And she was the last one left. I was lucky to find her."

Utterly clueless, and yet kind of adorable for it. She grabbed the kitten and raised it for a look before it went off the edge of the table. She palpated its belly, legs, checked its private bits and cleared her throat. "So how important is the sex of your cat?"

He frowned finally. "What do you mean?"

"Your girl is a boy."

His brows just about shot off his forehead. "Say what? A boy? Impossible. I checked between the legs myself. Nothing there."

"Yet. The balls haven't dropped."

"My princess is a prince?" His utter astonishment almost made her laugh.

"Maybe. I can only speak to the testicles it has."

"A boy. Hunh. So, gonna assume the food is the same?"

She nodded. "The only real difference in male or female is the operation they get. Spay or neuter."

His hand dropped to his groin. A reaction many men had to the neutering bit. "Must we cut them off?"

"Your little boy will turn into a pissing and noisy tom if you don't. Avoid neutering and you might find yourself the proud owner of a home marked in cat urine, not to mention granddaddy to a whole bunch of kittens."

The man's gaze widened. "Sorry, little guy. Guess you'll be getting the big snip."

"In better news, your kitten looks healthy. No sign of fleas or worms, but to be sure, you should bring in a stool sample and have it checked."

"You want me to poop in a jar?" He sounded utterly shocked. With reason.

She gaped. "Um, not your poop, the cat's!"

"Oh." He blushed but also grinned. "Guess that makes more sense."

Cute, but dumb. Shame.

"Would you like to do the second set of shots today?"

"Will it hurt?"

"It's a little pinch for the kitten and then lots of napping."

The Viking eyed the discarded beard and grabbed it, stuffing it into his pocket. "In case he needs comfort while he sleeps."

"You can hold the kitten to your chest while I do it," she offered.

The big man snuggled the tiny furball as she administered two shots, one in a haunch, the other in a shoulder. The cat barely noticed, but the man flinched each time.

She discarded the needles before removing her

gloves. "And that's it for this appointment. Shall we settle your bill and plan a date for the next?"

They emerged into the reception area, and she swung around the tall counter to log into the computer.

"Where's the dude that was handling the front?" he asked, looking around. The kitten slept in the front pocket of his lumberjacket.

"Francis? He's finished for the day." He'd left after whispering to her about the man with the bearded cat.

"You're by yourself? At night?" He sounded quite scandalized.

"Yes. I assure you I'm quite safe. Even vampires avoid me on account of my love for garlic."

"You can never have too much garlic," he agreed. "But that won't protect you if someone decides to target your place when you're alone. A friend of mine who works in a medical clinic a few blocks from here was recently accosted."

"I appreciate the concern, but you needn't worry about me. I'm a big girl." She could hold her own against most. She reached for a sheet she'd printed and handed it over. "Here's the bill for today."

He read it, and his expression grew more and more shocked. He whistled. "I am in the wrong business. Hot damn." He pulled out his credit card, and she finally saw his name. Ulric Bradbury. Francis hadn't created a file given they expected this to be a simple walk-in, one-time-only service.

"You should see the university bills." Between

those and the price tag attached to opening her own practice, she'd be working her ass off for a few more years yet before she could think of slowing down.

"I only ever did college. And that was a waste, given my degree in forestry is useless as a security guard."

"Surely a career in the environment is more lucrative."

"Not when I count the perks I get with my boss."

"Let's figure out your next appointment." She kept the tone businesslike as she finished off the visit. The receipt printed, and she handed it over.

"Thank you for choosing Honey's Vet Clinic for your pet. Have a great evening, Mr. Bradbury."

"I'll try." He marched to the door, only to pause and turn around as if to speak.

"Did you forget something?"

"I—Uh—No," he stammered before leaving.

But he'd be back.

In four weeks for the kitten's next set of shots.

3

You idiot! Ulric left the vet, kitten tucked in his pocket, confused and hesitant for once in his life.

He'd found the one. Would swear it. And yet she wore a wedding ring. Maybe to avoid guys hitting on her. Women did that in the bars all the time.

I should have asked her. Only wouldn't that come across as creepy? *Hey, so are you really married, or is that ring just for show?* He'd have earned a proper slap most likely. But how else could he find out if she was married and if yes, was she happy?

Not that a no answer would have made a difference. She wore a ring, making her off limits. Despite what he might have thought upon seeing her, she couldn't be the one.

Arriving home, he removed the groggy kitten from his pocket and placed him gently on the floor. He watched the little bugger saunter off.

The swagger should have been his first clue. Princess Froufrou, his first love, had always been so graceful and delicate. Unless you were late with her food, then claws unsheathed.

"What am I going to call you?"

"Meow." The reply didn't help.

At this time of night, there wasn't much to do other than game or watch television. Instead, he changed into a dark hoodie, locked his apartment, and returned to a spot near the clinic and waited. The lights inside remained bright. His watch indicated it was just after eight. She should be—

There she was. Dr. Honey Iris emerged, wearing a thick and warm Sherpa-lined jacket, not once looking to see if anyone lurked nearby. She locked the door and then strode off, handbag in hand, pace brisk.

He shadowed, and no this wasn't stalking. He wanted to ensure she made it home safe. Not once did she glance over her shoulder. Never noticed the bums in the alleys who turned their gazes in her direction. The cars that slowed as she passed.

No one confronted or accosted her, but the danger couldn't have been clearer. And where was her husband? Obviously not at home given the brick two-story townhouse she turned into had no lights on. She used her keys to get inside, and only then did windows illuminate in the two-story. Main floor, probably the living areas. Top the bedrooms.

Not that the layout mattered. Explain then why he

circled around the building to see the yard. Fences enclosed each postage-stamp-sized outdoor space. He vaulted them until he reached hers.

Gravel. No grass. A single chair on paving stones. The barbecue barely enough to cook two proper steaks. Not exactly the setting of a married couple.

He really should go home. His curiosity, obviously rubbing off from his kitten, had him wanting to see more. Who was the man who'd swept in and stolen the woman meant to be his mate?

The light at the rear of the house—usually the kitchen—remained off, the soft glow coming from the front. He crept up the porch steps and huddled by the barbecue as he glanced in. Definitely crossing the line into stalker zone.

The kitchen didn't really stand out. Basic wooden shaker cabinets painted white, black stone counters, gray ceramic floor. Three stools at the big island. No table or chairs, though. Standing, he could see past the kitchen into the middle space—a dining room by the looks of it—and past it a couch with a woman curled on it, a bowl in her lap as she snacked.

As if sensing his stare, she turned to look, and he ducked so fast he almost gave himself whiplash. He leaped from the deck and over the fence. Just in time, as her door slid open and she peeked outside.

He didn't breathe until it shut.

What am I doing?

Being crazy. Totally, and yet that didn't stop him from going home and giving his buddy Dorian a shout.

"Hey, I need you to look someone up for me," Ulric asked. He didn't worry about their conversation being overheard or tapped. Dorian was the tech guy for the Ottawa Valley Pack. Super smart dude and always willing to give a hand so long as it involved typing and not manual labor.

"What's up? Are we playing vigilante again?"

Ulric had a thing against crime. Sometimes if Billy and his cop buddies didn't do enough, Ulric and Quinn stepped in.

"Actually, I need info on a woman."

"Dare I ask why?"

"You'll laugh."

"You know laughter is the best medicine."

Ulric sighed. "You're such a dick. Fine then, I think I met the one."

"That's great, only you don't sound excited. What's wrong with her?"

"Nothing. She's gorgeous and smart. Married—"

"Wait, she's got a husband?" Dorian killed himself chuckling long enough that Ulric grumbled.

"Not funny. I'm traumatized that my one chance at a mate has been taken from me."

"Maybe she's not happily married."

"Doesn't matter. I can't exactly seduce her. It's not right."

"Sorry, dude. If she's off-limits, why the search?"

"I'm a masochist. I want to see who she's hitched to."

Ulric texted her name and clinic address over. Dorian did his magic, giving a running commentary as he dug up the dirt.

"Your girl is second-generation Canadian. Her parents immigrated here from Norway. She is thirty-five years old, making her a little older than you." Ulric had just turned thirty-three.

"Skip to the good parts."

"Everything in due time. She graduated with honors from high school and university. She is still paying off her student loans but would have been done if she'd not opened her business right when the COVID pandemic started. The lockdown gave her a beating, judging by her financials."

"Guess we were lucky Griffin's shop did so well." The Lanark Leaf's pot sales had flourished and not dropped since. "Now can we get to her husband."

"I've got a marriage certificate showing she married a Rocko Dieter right out of high school."

"High school sweethearts?" And still together. That didn't bode well.

"Hold on, they weren't married for long. He died."

"Wait, what?" Ulric straightened, which led to the suddenly woken kitten climbing his leg and clinging to the jean fabric over his crotch. His dick shrank tight in protection.

"Dieter died not long after she graduated with her

vet degree. Freak accident at work. He fell into some vat. According to news sources, his body was never recovered, as it disintegrated."

"Yikes. That's awful." It had also happened a decade before. "So, she's a widow. Does her social media show her dating? Does she have a profile on one of the matchmaking services?"

"I'm showing a few deactivated ones. She appears to be single at the moment. Pet free as well."

"This is amazing news," Ulric gushed.

The doctor was available and back in the running as his one and only. Now he just had to see her again. But how without looking desperate or stalkerish? After all, he wasn't supposed to know her husband died. His next appointment for the kitten now purring tucked between his neck and shoulder wasn't for four weeks.

That was when his gaze fell on the plastic jar for poop. Cat poop, not his, a mistake that still embarrassed. Way to sound suave. She must think him an utter idiot.

Now to wait for his little man to drop a load. As if the little furball knew he stalked his bowel movements, he wouldn't go. Ulric went to bed and woke in the morning to dried-out, gravel-covered poop. It wasn't until almost noon—because Ulric took the day off to watch for a fresh stool—after a morning of running and climbing—usually Ulric's leg—the kitten staggered to its litterbox and unleashed the most horrifying mess.

There was gagging. Even a tear, as the noxious

fumes watered his eyes. But the poop the size of his baby finger, surely too large for his little boy, made it inside the container safely.

His cat appeared unimpressed by the feat and slept in Ulric's left running shoe. Given his boots had a hole and it rained outside, it left only his rubber thong sandals, which usually only saw the gym.

He sat on the couch and waited.

And waited.

It wasn't until he got hungry and entered the kitchen at one that the cat came flying, throwing himself at Ulric's leg and climbing with a fierce meow.

"Calm down, terror. I'll feed you. Just give me a second."

"Meow." The less-than-patient reply.

The face dove into the plastic container before he could even think of dumping it. No sharp edges at least, so Ulric left him at it. Then, since his shoe was no longer hostage, he shoved his feet into them. Waited for the little porker to finish and sway with food fatigue. Then he carried him to the bed he'd placed by the window, where a spot of sunshine was about to hit.

Only then did he leave with his poop. He brown-bagged it, aware he carried feces. Given he could smell it, it surprised him he didn't get dirty looks. The stench permeated everything.

Focus on more pleasant things. Like Honey. He couldn't have asked for a more perfect match. A few inches shorter than him, meaning he wouldn't hurt himself bending over to kiss her. She might even tolerate some rougher tumbling. Those lips of hers had him tugging one out the night before as he imagined them wrapped around his cock.

Sucking. Hollowing those cheeks. Her hands gripping his ass as she—

Someone bumped into the arm holding the poop. The swinging of the brown bag brought him back to reality. Wrong time and place to be thinking about that, not to mention, hadn't he jerked enough since yesterday? He'd done three this morning alone.

Speaking of alone...

As he arrived at the clinic, the man who sat at the reception desk emerged. Francis had a lunch bag in one hand, book in the other. He was probably headed for the park and its benches. There wouldn't be many more days for eating outside as the fall waned and winter came sneaking in. They'd been seeing Christmas stuff since August.

Obscene. Especially since he had no one to decorate for but himself. But this year...it would all change. He had a cat and if he played this poop right, maybe the woman of his dreams.

With her receptionist off for lunch, now would be the perfect time. As he entered, a chime rang, indicating the door had opened.

"Hi, give me just a second and I'll be right with you."

Hearing her voice had him stepping closer to the

counter to glance over it. The lovely doctor punched away on a keyboard.

She lifted her head and opened her mouth, shut it, then said, "Hello, Mr. Bradbury. You shaved."

He had. It meant she saw his dimple as he said, "Call me Ulric. I brought the sample." He placed the brown bag on the counter.

"Thanks." She went back to typing.

He had to say something. "It's the cat's poop. Not mine."

"Good."

This wasn't going well. He had to recover. He drawled, "How you doing?" Oh no. he didn't.

He did. He said it in the Joey voice.

Her head lifted. She wore glasses today, plastic rimmed, big on her face and drooping on her nose. He wanted to kiss the tip of it so badly.

"I'm fine. Was there something else, Mr. Bradbury?"

He was losing her. What could he say? Admit he'd searched her out online? No, she'd think him a creep. Still, he couldn't just leave. "I see you wear a wedding ring. Have you been married long?"

"Since I was eighteen."

"Lucky guy."

"Who says it's a guy?"

He gaped. Her being a lesbian hadn't come up during the research. "Um, sorry. I made a very rude assumption."

Her lips curved. "That's okay. I'm just messing with you. The ring I wear is from my high school sweetheart. He spent an entire summer saving up for it." She held out her hand.

"Oh?" He tried to not sound too excited as she was about to come clean.

"Are you married?" she asked instead of telling him she was super available.

"No. Although I'd like to be." He tried a winsome smile.

"I hope you find the right woman or man to make you happy," she said with a straight face even as she stood right in front of him.

Did she not realize they were meant to be? The certainty vibrated within him.

"Are you happy?" Once more, he spoke without thinking.

Her lips turned down. "I'm afraid that's none of your business, Mr. Bradbury."

"Call me Ulric."

"That wouldn't be appropriate."

Because she wanted to persist in making him believe she was married. He couldn't contain himself. It blurted out from him. "I know you're a widow!"

"And?" She arched a brow. "I don't see as how it's any of your business."

She'd stumped him there. "It's not. It's just you're very attractive and I'd like to get to know you. Hopefully well enough I stop shoving my foot in my mouth every time I open it. I swear I'm not usually this dumb."

"I'm sure you're a lovely person. However, what you're suggesting isn't possible."

"You're seeing someone," he stated, doing his best to mask his disappointment.

"My refusal is because you're a client. As such, I cannot have a relationship with you. My father always says to never mix business with pleasure."

Damn her for having morals. The quickest solution had him saying, "I'm not your client anymore. I'm taking my poop elsewhere." He reached for the jar, but she snatched it too. Their hands connected and knocked the bag over. The bottle slipped out. They both watched in horror as it arced and then began coming back down.

He dove low.

She went high over the desk and grabbed it first but then couldn't control her descent.

When she came down, he provided the cushion. She landed atop him, poop jar held aloft.

"Good catch," he murmured as she squirmed over him. It took every ounce of gentleman in him to hold his erection in check.

"My dad always wanted a boy. He got me instead."

"Boys are overrated. I speak from experience." He wished he'd done less to stress his mother growing up. Every time he came home with bruises, broken bones, or needed stitches had been just one more stressor on her weak heart. She died before even reaching fifty.

Honey rolled over until she hit the floor then kneeled. "That was more excitement than I needed. And unprofessional of me too. I'm sorry. Here's your poop. Take it where you'd like."

He didn't grab the jar, opting to say instead, "What I'd like is for you to be my kitten's doctor but also come with me to dinner."

"Why are you being so insistent?" she asked as she stood.

"Because you are the woman of my dreams." This time his wayward tongue managed something that made her blush.

"You're just saying that."

"I'm serious. Come to dinner with me."

"Just dinner?"

"Yes." The more would come later after they'd savored some dating that left them both yearning.

"Let's say hypothetically that I said yes. You'd be okay if we each drive our own car?"

"Most definitely."

"Dinner doesn't mean you get to ask for sexual favors."

"I would never." He couldn't help but sound indignant.

"And if dinner doesn't work out, you'll take your business elsewhere."

"Agreed." He'd have said yes to anything for the chance.

"Very well. Dinner. Seven tomorrow night. I'll email you the address."

A take-charge woman. Could she get any hotter?

4

Why had she agreed? Ulric the Viking with a soft spot for cats was domineering and awkward at the same time. He complimented her with a fervor that flattered, but he also frightened.

There had to be something weird or wrong with him. A hunk of a guy like him wasn't going through a ton of trouble to be with someone like Honey.

Yet he'd apparently stalked her online. Not hard to do, it wasn't as if she'd hidden herself away. She was too boring to care what people saw or thought about her.

He'd sought her out, making it either super romantic or creepy. It would probably end up the latter, but just in case, she wanted to play it out because it would make a super cute meet-cute story.

Or she'd end up as a trophy that he'd skinned and stuffed for his collection.

She really should stop listening to those true crime podcasts.

Given she'd already agreed, might as well go through with it in a very public place. She'd told him she'd choose the venue. Only one place would do. Scivoloso Spaghetti, an Italian restaurant with the most incredible handmade pasta and sauces. She could eat to her heart's content and even bring some home. It was also cheap enough she could cover it in case her date didn't work out. Having been dined and ditched in the past, she'd learned her lesson: Never go anywhere she couldn't afford.

Francis noted her distraction late afternoon. "What's got you watching the clock?"

"I've got a date." An almost embarrassing admission. Usually, the prospect wouldn't have her so nervous.

That had Francis staring for a good second. "You?"

He well knew her saga when it came to dating. Her misadventures were part of the reason she'd started wearing her wedding ring again, just to remind herself that, once upon a time, someone had loved her enough to want to marry her.

"Yes. And I'm now second-guessing that decision."

"No. Don't you dare talk yourself out of it. About time you put yourself out there again."

"Easy for you to say." Francis had it so easy when it came to his husband, who also happened to be a former client...

Hmm. Maybe she should rethink her rules.

"Who is the lucky fellow?"

"The big guy with the kitten in his beard."

It took a lot to shock Francis. His mouth rounded, and then he yodeled, "Well hot damn. You snared yourself a hottie. Why are you still here? Go!" Francis came around the counter to shoo her.

She shook her head. "It's only four. We don't close for another hour."

"You're done with your appointments for the day."

"There could be an emergency walk-in." Another Ulric with a pet problem.

"You're not the only vet in town. Go. Vamoose. *Allez-y*."

In the end, Francis made it impossible to argue. She left, practically jogging home, resisting an urge to glance over her shoulder, feeling as if she were watched. Not the first time this week. But she refused to give in to paranoia. She had a date. It made her rather giddy.

She quickly showered and spent time mowing her armpits and legs. It meant she didn't have enough time to fully dry her hair. The curse of long tresses. She bound it in a braid that she coiled in a bun and jabbed with two sticks. She tugged a few wisps out to frame her face, which she lightly coated with makeup. She kept her look natural. It suited her best. She'd tried the vamp look, and it made her giggle. Bright red lipstick didn't suit her style.

She paired the hair and face with a simple sweater dress in a navy blue. Casual, yet fancy enough for a night out. It hugged her curves and didn't conceal her sturdy nature. She didn't have a tiny waist men could span with their hands, but she was well proportioned. Big hips and tits, as one guy had said upon meeting her. The same one who left her with the bill after ordering all the most expensive items.

Ulric called me beautiful. And she didn't get the impression he'd lied. There'd been genuine admiration in his gaze.

The reminder brought a flush of heat. It happened every time he came to mind. Would tonight be the night she broke another rule about not having sex on a first date?

She had shaved...

But one-night stands weren't usually her thing. She didn't know this Ulric well enough to hazard a guess if they'd make it to dessert, let alone to another outing.

Lastly, she threw on a simple silver pendant and matching earrings. She then eyed her hand and the ring on it. A ring she wore when life got her down. A reminder of better days. She slipped it off and tucked it into her jewelry box. Living in the now meant not clinging to the past.

On the walk over to the restaurant—which was actually only one street over from her place—she again felt watched. This time she did glance over and thought she saw someone ducking into the flower shop.

Since when did she succumb to paranoia? No one was stalking her.

She continued to the restaurant, where she was greeted by the hostess, Maria, with a hearty, "Dr. Iris. So nice to see you back."

It didn't matter how many times she told Maria to call her Honey, the woman insisted ever since she'd saved her pet parakeet. He'd been losing his feathers along with his appetite. Once Maria got him a companion, on Honey's advice, things improved.

"I've got your regular table ready."

It was as Maria grabbed only one menu that Honey cleared her throat to say, "Table for two tonight, please. I am meeting someone."

Maria paused. "A man?"

She nodded. Maria tucked the regular menu back and grabbed two of the special ones.

"Then tonight you get the chef's table."

It meant being tucked into a window alcove close to the kitchen and yet apart from everything. It was intimate, and she almost said no until his deep voice shivered her from behind.

"I hope I'm not late."

She whirled, only to find him right there. Her eyes were level with his mouth. She lifted her gaze.

His lips quirked. "Hi."

"Hi," she said awkwardly. "You're early."

"Not really since you're here."

Maria stared up, jaw dropped, then squeaked,

"You're her date. Mama mia. Dr. Iris is getting a fever tonight." Maria turned to lead them with a giggle.

Honey just wanted to die of embarrassment. No way did Ulric not grasp the innuendo.

"This place smells incredible. I can't wait to try it." He then placed his hand lightly in the middle of her back as she walked—or floated, hard to tell—to their table.

He sat across from her, yet the table wasn't big enough to keep his knees from bumping into hers. Every single time, she felt a tingle.

Given this was a night for breaking rules. When Maria returned with the wine list, rather than her customary no thank you, Honey pointed. "I'll have a glass of Chardonnay."

"Bring a bottle. This is my treat," Ulric added.

"You don't have to," Honey quickly interjected as Maria left. "We can go Dutch."

He snorted. "I asked you out."

"I chose the place."

"And I am super excited. Did I see correctly the pasta is freshly made?"

She nodded and launched into a mini history of the place. Maria's dad and uncle had started it more than forty years ago. Their children now ran most of it.

"That's awesome. I'm kind of in the family business too."

"Oh, what do you do?" she asked, taking a sip of wine.

"I provide security for a local pot shop."

She sprayed him with her beverage. "Oh my. Sorry. I don't—Uh." Embarrassed, she hastened to his side to pat him with a napkin.

He grabbed her wrist gently and murmured, "It's okay. Weed might be legal, but it's new enough lots of folks are taken by surprise by it."

"I didn't mean to imply by my reaction that I disapprove. It was just unexpected."

"What did you think I did?"

She'd not honestly thought of it. Eyeing him with his long hair, the clean-shaven jaw—which turned out to be square and perfect without his beard—wearing a button-up shirt tucked into jeans, she offered a lame, "Construction worker?"

He snorted. "While I can wield a hammer and screwdriver, I'm better at hand-to-hand combat and observation. Like for example, I know you come here often by the way Maria and one of the chefs keep checking on you."

"I love this place." An easy admission to make.

"And they obviously care for you. Meaning you're nice to people."

"Why would I be rude?"

"Believe it or not, some folks just can't help themselves."

"True," she admitted, having seen it herself with her practice. "What kind of guy are you?" she asked, even as she was getting a good idea.

"The kind that will move a sofa in the rain for a friend. Get a shovel if he says he's got a body."

"Sacrifice his beard for a cat?" she added.

"I'd shave my whole head if it meant I got to meet you."

The flattery brought heat to her cheeks, and she turned her head. "I'm not that special."

"To me you are."

All evening long, he'd drop comments along those lines. How he found her attractive. Sexy. Witty. He laughed at her dumb jokes. She laughed at his. They ended up sitting side by side for the shared dessert brought out by the beaming Chef Mario. No, his brother wasn't Luigi but Lorenzo.

He fed her bites, and when she licked her lips to capture a drop of sweetness, he stared so intently she flushed head to toe.

He lifted his hand and in a voice unsteady said, "Check, please."

Not only did he pay, he tipped well. Enough Maria told him to come again anytime. No reservation needed.

"I will so be going back," he groaned, rubbing his belly. "That was insanely good food. But even better company."

There he went again. So charming that when he said, "Let me walk you to your car," she replied, "I didn't drive. My place is only a block away. Care to come by for a nightcap?"

"I would love that."

Too late to retract the invitation. At the same time Honey didn't want the evening to end.

He tucked her hand in the crook of his arm as they strolled, the thickness of it impressive. She'd only had two glasses of wine and couldn't blame them for the heat flushing her body. Being near him had her in a state of awareness that defied all logic.

Then again, maybe not. He was damned sexy.

As they went up the steps to her place, she'd never been happier that she'd tidied a bit and changed her sheets. Because there was a really good chance they'd end up in bed.

The keys shook, making it hard to unlock the door. Her breath caught when his hand came over hers. He murmured against her ear, "Maybe I shouldn't come inside."

"Why not?"

"Because I want to kiss you very badly, which I know is bad form since this is our first date."

"What if I want you to kiss me?"

He groaned. "You're killing me here."

"Please don't die. I hear it's a ton of paperwork."

He chuckled. "Why are you so perfect?"

Why did he know exactly what to say? She leaned in and kissed him.

What she didn't expect was once their lips locked, she didn't want to stop.

5

ALL DINNER long Ulric had been doing his best to control his attraction for the woman across from him. She enraptured his every sense. Witty and funny, sexy as fucking hell.

She didn't hold back when it came to eating. Or laughing. If he asked her a question, she answered.

One of three kids. Her parents lived just outside of Ottawa. Her dad worked as a semi-retired accountant for a private company. Mom dabbled in the arts.

She had no kids, not even furbabies, at home. Which surprised him. As she'd explained, *"I have hundreds of pets with my practice."*

The surprise was on her. She'd just acquired a wolf. Not that he'd ever tell. In this moment, he was a man and she was a woman.

They kissed their way into the house, her lips parting before his tongue's insistence. No fear or hesitation. She flung her arms around his neck and hung on tight.

The sweetness of her tantalized. His hands roamed the fabric of her dress, the material molding her frame but a barrier to his touch. He kept kissing as he tugged at it, rolling it up her body and only interrupting their embrace to remove it completely, leaving her clad in a black lace bra and underwear.

"Damn." All he could say and yet she ducked her head.

Her arousal perfumed the air. He stripped his shirt before reaching for her and growling, "Come here."

Their lips meshed as his hands went exploring, following the slight indent of her spine down to the hollow above her ass. What an ass. He squeezed it, and she trembled.

He could have kissed her all night, but his mouth wanted to check out her flesh. He trailed his lips across her jawline to her earlobe. A hot blow of air and she moaned, sagging in his grip.

Mmm. He grabbed hold of her ear for a nibble, and she went entirely weak. Good thing there was a couch nearby. He sat her on it and continued his exploration, sliding his lips over her neck, feeling the rapid flutter of her pulse. His heartbeat just as fast.

The urge to bite had him dragging his teeth on her flesh, and she gasped, her body arcing into him.

Not yet. He had to go slow. He couldn't scare her.

He traced a path down to the valley between her

breasts, two heavy globes waiting for his touch. He nuzzled them, the skin silky soft, her nipples tempting buds. He pulled one into his mouth for a suck. She cried out, and so he tugged hard, tightening her bud and then switching to the other until it was just as taut. She moaned and writhed at his touch. He sucked and then gave a sample nibble. She bucked hard and cried out.

Not in pain. A flood, her arousal almost drove him insane.

He kissed his way down next over her belly then her mound. Not shaven, but natural the way he liked it. She parted her thighs for him, just as eager for what was about to come. He cupped her mound, feeling Honey's nectar waiting for him to taste.

He buried his face between her legs and swiped her cleft with his tongue. Her whole body went still except for her hands. They gripped his hair.

"More," she whispered.

Oh, he planned to. Her first orgasm would be on his tongue. He licked her again and again, gauging her excitement by how tightly those fingers gripped his hair. He kept swiping with his tongue, parting her nether lips, teasing her clit. The taste of her making him so fucking hard.

He wanted nothing more than to sink into her and thrust until she came around his cock. Soon. She was on the edge of her first orgasm.

His lips tugged at her clit before he lapped it with

frantic strokes. He managed to thrust two fingers into her. Her hips thrust against his face, and her channel clamped him hard. Faster and faster, his tongue circled and teased. His fingers went deep to find her sweet spot. She groaned and rotated her hands in time to his motions.

When she came, he felt it, tasted it, revelled in her powerful climax as she came and shouted his name. "Ulric!"

Oh, fuck yeah.

He kept teasing her until she whimpered. Only then did he stand to strip off his pants, condom packet in hand before they hit the floor.

To his pleasure, she reached out to help him put it on then dragged him to the couch. Once he sat, she stood and straddled him. Her swollen lips leaned in for a kiss as she maneuvered over his cock. Once more she grabbed him, drawing a groan. She guided him to her cleft, rubbing the head of him against her.

Then she sat down hard, and Ulric went rigid. She took him without qualm. Fisted him tight. And then she started to bounce.

He just about died. Any thoughts of finesse went out the window as he struggled to hold on as she rode him. A glorious beauty with bouncing tits, her head thrown back, skin flushed with pleasure.

He was going to come. Fuck. Not before she did. He wanted—

She came, and he did die. She clamped down so tight it was the most exquisite pleasure.

So intense he hugged her tight to him and his mouth latched to her neck. His teeth ached to mark, but he held on. It was too soon.

She collapsed against him and sighed. "That was fun."

"Just fun?" he growled. "Maybe we should start over."

She blinked at him. "Don't you need time to recover?"

Since she still sat atop him, she felt the difference as his cock said hello, ready for round two.

The sexiest of smiles stretched her lips. "Don't tell me I finally found a guy who can keep up."

A challenge if he ever heard one.

By the time they collapsed in her bed, he expected to wake with raw dick and a case of the sappy smiles.

Instead, he woke to the rude blaring of an alarm clock at the ungodly hour of six a.m.

6

"Argh!" Ulric buried his head under the pillow. "It's too early."

"For you maybe, but I have to work." She flipped back the covers, exposing his flank. A nice flank that she'd dug her nails into just the night before.

He groaned. "I work, too, just not so early."

"Go back to sleep. I'll be out of here in fifteen minutes."

It turned out to be thirty because he joined her in the shower, a tight fit given their size, but he made it work.

Oh boy did he ever. She bit her lip at the reminder.

He'd then proceeded to walk her to the clinic and kissed her soundly before promising to see her later.

Francis took one look at her face when he got in and declared, "You got laid."

"That sounds so basic for what I experienced." Ulric had taken sex to the next level.

"So does that mean you're a couple now?"

"I don't know." They'd talked all dinner long, but the subject of what they both wanted hadn't really been a part of it.

"Do you want to be his partner?"

"Maybe? It's too soon to tell. We just met." And had sex. Would this be a one-night stand? Or did he mean it when he said he'd see her later?

"Stop making excuses. You obviously like the man, and you're not getting any younger."

"Ouch, and I'll have you know the thirties aren't old. I'm not even halfway through my life expectancy."

"You need to get enjoying it before you are too old. Speaking of which, we had a cancellation at our cottage this weekend. Last one before we shut it down for the season. Did you and the new beau perhaps want to pay it a visit?"

"Ask him to go away? Seems a little fast."

"Says the girl who went all the way." Francis didn't pussyfoot around it. "The bed is extra sturdy, and if you're not bothered by the cold, the lake is empty of boaters this time of year, making it nice and calm for swimming."

"Maybe," she said, even as the idea percolated. She'd literally only met Ulric days ago. Had one epic date. One night of incredible sex. She couldn't even be sure he'd meant it about seeing her later. Most guys usually skipped a few days before calling back.

Ulric wasn't most guys.

He showed up at noon with a paper bag. She exited an examination room with Mrs. Garwosky and her Pomeranian to find him chatting with Francis.

Ulric turned a beaming smile at her. "There's my Honeybee. I noticed you didn't pack a lunch, so I brought you and Francis something from the sandwich shop close to where I work."

"Thank you." She neared him, awkward and not knowing what to do. Was she supposed to hug him? Kiss him? What if he wasn't into public displays of affection?

He solved the dilemma by reaching for her, his hand firm on her waist as he drew her close to give her a sound smooch on the lips and a murmured, "Sorry if I got impatient to see you."

Wait, he was apologizing? "Don't be silly. I'm glad you came." She smiled back at him and saw how his nostrils flared.

It occurred to her then what he probably thought of when she said "came," which led to her blushing and a satisfied male smile crossing his lips.

Francis cleared his throat. "It's getting hot in here. I'm going to eat my lunch in the park."

"Don't leave on my account," Ulric stated. "I can't stay. My break is almost over."

"What time do you finish work?" she asked.

"Seven, because as Quinn reminded me, I've been slacking off the last few days. And he's grumpy seeing as how I had him babysitting Terror last night and my boy might have been a tad bit rambunctious."

"I'm done at five and was going to hit the grocery store since my fridge is empty. Can I make you dinner?" she boldly offered.

"Hell yeah."

"Any special requests?"

"You on a plate?"

She just about combusted.

Francis, who'd remained behind the counter, coughed, and Ulric winked. "See you later," he added a firm kiss. Then he was gone, and she stared at the spot he'd stood in, trying to calm her racing heart.

Francis whistled. "Damn, but that man is into you."

"Do you think so?" Because she wanted to believe, even as she had a hard time. Ulric seemed too perfect. *Too* into her.

"That man couldn't keep his eyes off you. And he brought you food." Francis took off with his sandwich and left her to sit, eyeing hers. He'd gotten her a fresh twelve-inch Italian bun layered with ham, Swiss cheese, bacon, tomato, lettuce, and mayo.

Delicious. It gave her an idea for dinner.

He was at her door by seven twenty with a bottle of wine and a box of desserts. He then apologized. "Sorry

I didn't shower before coming over. I didn't want to make you wait."

"We can shower later when we're dirtier," she sassed. Not her usual kind of thing, and she felt a little dumb until he dragged her close and kissed her, growling against her mouth, "Don't tempt me before dinner because it's all I can do to not take you right here, right now."

"Why don't you?"

"Your dinner. It will burn."

"I turned off the oven," she whispered before her hands went to his pants.

He took her there in the front against the wall, lifting her so he could get the right angle, holding and bouncing her to an appetizer of what was to come.

Food. Sex. And then, because he sheepishly admitted he was worried about Terror being alone, since Quinn refused to kitten-sit two nights in a row, they dressed and walked to his place with an overnight bag for her.

Second date and not only was the sex even better, she slept over in his bed. Not exactly cuddled, as the kitten chose to wedge himself between them.

She smiled over the furry body at Ulric and said, "Francis said we could borrow his cottage next weekend. Think Terror is up for a road trip?"

"Hell yeah, he is!"

A few days later, Terror did not appreciate the car ride, but he did enjoy scouting out the new space, a space they didn't leave much. They spent their time making love.

And it was love. Ulric said it quite clearly that first night there. "I am falling in love with you, Bee."

Some might have been freaked by this declaration, even rushed. Her?

"Ditto," was her blushed reply. How she still had any heat to give her cheeks after all they'd done…

The following week, they got their bloodwork done and, because she used an IUD, ditched the condoms.

She didn't expect a difference.

Wrong. The sex went next level the first time they went at it bare-skinned.

Thrust, slide. The pleasure of it had her gasping and crying out. Her nails dug into his back. Her lips latched on to him, sucking and leaving a mark that turned into a bite as her orgasm hit. She bit hard enough she tasted metal.

Apparently, Ulric didn't mind because that was when his hips went rigid, burying his cock, and he howled. An eerie sound cut off when he buried his mouth against her flesh and returned the bite.

The sharp pain of it should have distracted. Instead it rolled her into a second climax that left her breathless and sightless for a moment. A literal orgasm blackout.

She would have basked in the glow forever if he'd not said, "Move in with me."

"No." She didn't even hesitate. She really liked

Ulric. Likely even loved. But they'd been dating less than a month.

"We spend every day and night together." With Terror commuting between their places.

"We do, but we're in the honeymoon phase. What if it wears off and you realize you want your space?"

"My love for you isn't fickle," he argued.

"It's also shiny and brand new," she argued, trying to remain pragmatic.

"You're afraid I'm going to leave."

"It's been a pattern my whole life, so, yes, I'm going to be cautious." Said by the woman who'd slept with him on her first date.

"We're meant to be together," he insisted.

"Then in that case you won't mind waiting a little bit. For me," she added.

He sighed. "If I must."

To ease his disappointment, she gave him some hope. "If I do eventually say yes, it will be my place simply because it's bigger."

He grinned. "Do I get to bring my comfy chairs and game system?"

"If we do move in together, it will be just as much your place as mine. You can even choose some colors to repaint some rooms. Just not the kitchen. That's where I draw the line."

"You can do all the decorating so long as I'm the guy wielding the paintbrush and rolling his eyes at his Honey-do list."

"Does that Honey-do list include doing me?"

It did. Apparently, a daily recurring task that brought them both great pleasure.

Every day became exciting. Her life full of laughter, love, and happiness.

So explain the dread that it was all about to end.

7

HAPPINESS FILLED ULRIC. He and Honey meshed together like mustard on a hotdog with onions, mayo, and relish. Given how well it had been going, he wouldn't take her refusal to move in as a setback. She didn't yet realize they were soul mates. She just needed a little more time.

Ulric had waited his whole life to meet the one. He could be patient a while longer. Since he'd spent the night at her place, he brought Terror with him to work. The cat was actually a source of amusement with the Pack. They might laugh at his choice in pet, and yet they all doted on the little feline who had free reign of the store.

Until Tyrone walked in. His dozens of swinging braids with their beads proved too much temptation for a young kitty who fancied himself an agile hunter. He wasn't. Terror missed his ambitious jumps more often than he made them, but once he latched onto something—say like one of Tyrone's braids—then he held on for dear life.

Good thing Tyrone was chill about it. The discount on his weed purchase probably helped.

Just after Ulric's midday lunch drop-off to Honey—where he stole a kiss and a grope that left her flushed—Griffin called him into his office, aka the living room in his apartment over the store. Maeve was doing a shift at the hospital, so it was just his boss and a stranger who must have come up via the back staircase.

They sat on couches that faced each other. His boss, Griffin Lanark—a dark-haired dude with creeping grays—sat on one and across from him a woman, her hair cut fairly short but spiked on top, the tips frosted. Her nose and ears were pierced. She wore all black: jeans, sweater, socks. The combat boots on the shoe mat must be hers too.

"Hey, boss," Ulric offered as greeting. "You hollered?"

"I did. Ulric, I want you to meet Doctor Silver."

"Nice to meet you." He held out his hand, and she extended a gloved one to grip. She had a firm grasp and eyed him quite frankly with eyes a little closer to golden yellow than brown. There was something off about her scent. Something even the heavy coconut mist she'd sprayed couldn't hide.

She released his hand and eyed him, saying, "He's

a fit specimen like most of your Pack. How long since the change?"

Wait what? Ulric recoiled.

Griffin didn't seem phased. "More than ten years now."

"Meaning he has well-established Lycan genetics."

Ulric finally interrupted. "Hold on, what's happening here? Why are you telling her about, you know, *the secret*?" He added finger quotes.

"Doctor Silver is here as part of a nationwide venture to learn more medically about our kind. For some reason, very little study has been done, but Doctor Silver aims to change that."

"And you're just telling her everything. Is that wise?" The Lycan secret was a well-guarded one, even as it got harder and harder to hide with social media in everyone's business these days.

"He's not telling me anything I don't already know about the Lycan people. Rest assured, my interest in the community is purely scientific." Her voice emerged as a husky murmur.

"Said every mad doctor and government hack," Ulric muttered with a scowl.

"I can only state that I am neither of those. I truly want to understand more about the Lycan condition."

"Why?"

"Because we won't be able to keep it secret forever," she said, echoing his recent thought.

"And how does studying us help?"

"Because the Lycan community will need to counter misinformation and superstition when they end up revealed."

"We're good at hiding."

It was Griffin who interjected. "Our days of hiding are almost over. Dorian says for every story or sighting they squash, another crops up. Soon we won't be able to stop one going viral."

"In which case someone will debunk it as a hoax." They'd done it before. When a werewolf went rabid, they left a trail that was hard to ignore.

"Do you want to be a part of the research or not?" Griffin asked.

"Maybe. What are her qualifications?"

The doctor shook her head. "If you're going to be difficult, this won't work. Do you have someone else I can talk to?" The last directed at Griffin.

"Yeah, Quinn might be cool with it. Dorian, though, will never agree. He's a got a thing about staying anonymous."

"Hold on a second, I never said no, but I do have questions," Ulric argued. "Starting with, how come you didn't run this through security first? How do you know she's legit?"

"Because Doctor Silver was vouched for by Theo Russell." The alpha of the Toronto Golden Paw Pack. "She tested quite a few in his Pack but needs more samples for comparison as part of her work for the Cabal."

The Cabal. The word so rarely spoken froze him.

"She's a Cabal agent?" he whispered, despite her sitting right there.

She rolled her eyes. "For god's sake, they're not the bogeyman. And, yes, I was hired by the Cabal. Who are Lycan like you, I might add."

"I know who they are." The Cabal's job on a worldwide level involved watching over the Packs. They only rarely got involved, but when they did, shit happened. A Pack being indiscreet often resulted in some or all the adults disappearing as a lesson to follow the rules.

The Cabal didn't fuck around, meaning if they wanted this woman running tests, then saying no wasn't a real option.

"Why didn't you say that in the first place?" Ulric grumbled. "When do we start?"

"Tomorrow. Your Alpha will give you the address. Tell no one where you're going or what you're doing. It will involve you spending three nights for sleep monitoring, so make arrangements, as you won't be able to leave once we start."

"What about phone calls? My girlfriend will think it's weird if I don't call."

"You will be able to contact people so long as you remain discreet."

"Can I bring my cat?"

"No."

Griffin coughed. "I'm sure me and the boys can take care of him for a few days."

"I'll ask Honey first and see what she says." Honey, whom he'd have to leave for three days. "I better being getting paid for this," he grumbled. "Terror is a growing boy." Not to mention he had his eye on a ring.

"You'll be paid. And as a bonus, take the rest of the day off to clear out your fridge and tell your girlfriend you'll be gone."

"What am I supposed to tell her?" Ulric sucked at lying.

"It's not that hard," Dr. Silver interjected. "Your boss is having problems with a shipment and has sent someone on his security team to travel with it."

"You want me to tell her I'm going away for a few days as a drug mule?"

Dr. Silver shrugged. "I really don't care what excuse you use."

In the end, by the time he arrived at Honey's work to walk her home, he realized Silver's lie would probably work best. "I gotta go out of town for a few days. Boss thinks someone is shorting our shipments in transit."

"I'll miss you," she said. "Want me to watch Terror for you?"

She took it too well.

"You're not sad I'm leaving?"

"Of course I am, but at the same time, it might be good because I think I'm coming down with something." She put a hand to her stomach. "Be warned, if I'm sick, it's probably already too late for you."

"I've got the constitution of a wolf." He thumped his chest.

She snorted. "You're more like a giant bear."

"I'm insulted."

"Does that mean no more bear hugs?"

He grinned. "Like hell." He grabbed her in one that swept her off her feet.

"Put me down."

She did look green.

He carried her to bed, and Terror snuggled in beside her. When he would have joined them, she waved a hand. "Go. You probably have to pack. I'll be fine."

"It doesn't feel right leaving you while you're sick."

"I'll be fine. I've ridden out many colds and flus on my own. At worst, I can call my mom for one of her vile remedies."

"I'll call you every day, at least twice."

Then, despite her protests, he kissed her.

Missed her as he tossed and turned in his lonely bed. It was only for a few days. The next morning when he called, she said she felt better and was already at work.

With no excuse, he headed for the address Griffin made him memorize.

"This is like super-secret spy stuff," he'd joked.

Griffin didn't disagree.

Wild shit.

The place was a former restaurant with for lease signs plastered all over it. Odd place to be doing medical tests. Then again, no one would ever know.

The doctor herself let him inside, and he was surprised to see she worked alone.

"No nurse assistant?" he asked.

"I prefer to do the work myself to ensure no errors are made."

A control freak who lacked personality, as she literally ran him like a rat in a wheel. In this case a treadmill. He spent that first day being measured as he exercised.

Electrodes all over his body tracked everything. Heart rate, temperature, sweat. So much sweat.

As he jogged for the fourth time that day, and she stood watching with her tablet, he asked, "Are our bodies that much different from the unbitten?" Calling them human felt dumb. He was human, just with a little something extra.

"Physically, no, or Lycans would have been hard to hide all this time. But on a cellular and genetic level, there appear to be markers that indicate Lycan, but at the same time, they're not all the same. I'm trying to form a baseline for them."

"How is it you know about us? Are you married to a Lycan?"

"Nope. But I've been aware of them for a while. And since I'm sure you won't shut up unless I tell you why"—she shoved up her sleeve past the edge of her gloves to show the scars on her forearm—"I was attacked by a werewolf while at university."

"What?" The very idea horrified.

"It happened on a full moon. I was working on a university project with my lab partner. He shifted suddenly and attacked me. I spent months in the hospital in a coma. When I woke, one of the Cabal was there to tell me I had a choice. I could come and work for them and crack the secret of Lycanthropy, or I could die and take my secret with me."

"Not much of a choice."

"No, but that wasn't their fault. The fact a rogue wolf escaped detection was. Hence the reason why I even got a choice."

"Did they catch the guy who attacked you?"

"They did. He was executed for his crimes. Now, if we're done..." She pushed a button, and he had to sprint to keep up on the treadmill.

That evening, he slept on the cot set up where tables and chairs used to seat patrons. He'd eaten a high carb dinner and been measured some more.

He eventually managed to call Honey. No video, though, so she didn't see his location.

She answered with a perky, "Hey, handsome."

"How's my Honeybee?"

"Missing you, but don't worry. Terror is determined to take your place. He's keeping my crotch warm."

"Lucky."

"How's your work going?"

"Fine. Wishing I was with you, though." Then, because he was a guy, he asked, "What are you wearing?"

"My sexy T-shirt that says Bigfoot is my daddy." She laughed.

And despite their distance apart, he smiled.

"How was your day?"

They spoke for more than hour, and he might have talked longer, but she yawned.

"Good night, my Viking."

"Love you," he murmured.

"Love you more," she taunted before she hung up.

Argh. Why did he have to be here on a stupid cot instead of snuggled by her side?

The rude awakening at two a.m. via bullhorn sat him bolt upright, heart pounding.

Silver stood at the foot of his cot taking notes.

"What the fuck!"

"Checking your startle reflex. Go back to sleep." No apology, she just turned and walked off. As for sleep, it happened with one eye open.

The next day was more exercise, along with samples being taken. A needle led to vial after vial of blood being drawn. Hair was snipped. Skin scraped. Even incised. At the end, she handed him two jars.

"Pee in the one with the yellow lid. Ejaculate in the white."

He blinked at them. "You want me to fill them?"

"Yes you, because I am not holding your dick for you while you squirt."

"I wasn't suggesting..." he stammered.

"You know where the bathroom is."

He trudged over. Peeing was fine. He had to go. But the other? He'd not masturbated since meeting Honey. It felt wrong to do it clandestinely in that bathroom. It helped that he thought of Honey.

He emerged and handed over the bottles, only to blush as she whistled. "Damn, that's quite the load. You sure you're shooting blanks?"

The very idea. "I'm a big guy," was his embarrassed retort. "Not sure why you need it seeing as how I've been fixed for years." A vasectomy was required of all who became Lycan given pregnancy killed.

"Word is you have samples on ice from before the change."

He nodded. "While I wasn't sure about the whole kid thing, I wanted the option just in case I changed my mind later." Having met Honey, he was glad he'd had the forethought. The thought of Honey swelling with his child...

He missed her something fierce.

It was a long four days. Phone calls barely cut it. It didn't help Honey had begged off early on a few, still feeling off kilter.

Don't worry, Honeybee. He was coming home

today, and he'd wait on her hand and foot until she shook off the bug.

He made it to her place just before supper. He didn't even have to knock.

Honey flung open the door and welcomed him with a wide smile. "Ulric!" she squealed and threw herself at him.

But when he would have hugged her tight and spun, she protested.

"No twirling unless you want to wear my last meal."

"Still feeling ill?"

"Yes and no. I've got some exciting, if shocking, news."

"What is it?"

"So I know we didn't talk about it, mostly because it should have been impossible, only it appears my IUD must have gotten flushed out."

The more she spoke, the colder he got.

Until he was a frozen cube as she finally blurted out, "I'm pregnant."

8

"Excuse me?" Ulric wavered on his feet after her announcement, his expression a mask of shock.

"I'm pregnant," Honey repeated, even as she realized she took a chance telling him.

Things between her and Ulric had been amazing thus far. A gentle giant who had his alpha-male moments. Holding doors open. Taking out the garbage. Paying every time they went out. He had old-school manners in that respect. But he wasn't just about doing his part. He seemed obsessed with her pleasure, making her orgasm like nothing she'd imagined. Sex with him had her eager for the next time they were together. Just one look and she was ready. And even better it appeared to be the same for him. He touched her almost constantly. They snuggled for television time. In bed. Walked hand in hand. He was so perfect she waited for the other shoe to drop.

It emerged as puke instead.

She hated vomiting, but it happened the same day he left on his trip. She popped some ginger, and it somewhat settled her stomach. But after four days of it, and with no other symptoms, she ruled out a virus and doubted she suffered from lingering food poisoning, which left one possibility.

On the way to work, she'd hit a pharmacy and bought a pregnancy test. She smuggled it into the bathroom without Francis seeing, and her hand shook as she peed on the strip.

It couldn't be true. She had an IUD and it was only two years old, so not even close to expired. But even IUDs weren't 100%. They could dislodge or even exit the body without warning.

She washed her hands and while waiting for the result did an intimate grope to see if she could touch the string for her device. Cervix, check. String... Uh-oh. She might have been worried if she felt pain or cramping, the signs of a dislodged unit, but given her last heavy period, she suspected her body had flushed it out without her knowing.

The IUD had been their line of defense against pregnancy. Although, it should be noted, she'd mostly gotten it because it thinned her periods, and it wasn't like she was in a committed relationship where she wanted kids. What if she was pregnant?

The question repeated itself as she waited. She waffled between excitement because she'd always wanted to be a mom and fear because she didn't know how Ulric would react.

Given how he stood rigid and blank faced, he wasn't pleased. "You're pregnant?" he repeated, his tone flatter than she'd ever heard.

"Not on purpose," she hastened to add. "I had an IUD that's supposed to stop that kind of thing, only it must have slipped out, and, well, you and I have been quite active." She blushed.

"You're sure of this? It's not some other medical issue."

"I confirmed it with my office ultrasound machine. There's a peanut growing in there." Seeing it had her trembling. Because, in that moment, she knew, no matter what, she was having this baby.

Apparently alone as he coldly asked, "Who's the father?"

The question snapped her head like a slap. "You are of course."

"That's impossible. I'm sterile."

She gaped at him. "It has to be you because you're the only man I've been with."

Pain flashed on his face, followed by anger. "Obviously not or you wouldn't be carrying someone else's child."

"I'm not. Who said you were sterile?" she shouted, getting mad at the accusation.

"The doctor who performed the vasectomy."

"You're neutered?" How had this never come up in conversation? She couldn't help but blurt out, "Why?"

"Because I can't have kids."

"You don't want a family?" There went her dream. It shattered in an instant.

"Never said that. I got some junk frozen in case I found someone. And let me tell you right now, I didn't defrost any to turkey baster you with. So don't even try to claim I did."

"Seriously?" she snapped. "Do you see me as that desperate? Well, I have news for you. I'm not. The only thing I did was stupidly have unprotected sex with you. Should have known better. Does this mean your STD panel was a lie too?"

"I'm not the liar here," he seethed.

"Neither am I. And quite honestly, I don't think I like you right now. You need to leave."

"I want to know who he is." Violence seethed from his pores. His anger all too real. He really thought the worst of her.

It broke her heart.

"Then look in a mirror because, whatever you might think, it appears as if your vasectomy has reversed itself because this is your baby. But don't worry, I won't come after you for child support," she spat.

"As if I'd pay. One paternity test—"

"Will prove it."

"Indeed, it will," he muttered as he stalked out the door.

Left and he didn't return. Not that night. Nor the next morning.

A stunned Honey wondered how she could have been so dumb. He'd made her believe he loved her. Made her feel so damned special. And then to play the aggrieved victim...

How dare he?

"Don't worry, peanut," she whispered to her belly. "We're better off without him."

In his misplaced ire, he'd forgotten his cat. Good. Because Honey had bonded with Terror. They'd even come to an understanding. She'd not put him in the cage to carry to work if he let her put on the harness on him and he sat on her shoulder, his leash wrapped around her hand, just in case.

That day at work she kept expecting to see Ulric. The coward instead texted to inform her he'd be swinging by the house to pick up his cat.

She texted back. *No.*

Why not? Terror is mine.

So is this baby. Guess what, I'm keeping both.

She then blocked his number. Eyed the clock and gathered the cat and her things. "Francis, I'm leaving early."

"Hot date?"

"Not exactly." She'd not told him of the breakup. It helped she'd not yet cried. Anger sustained her.

Until her mother opened the door to her childhood home.

Then she burst in tears.

9

After Honey's heart-rending announcement, Ulric went home and got drunk. The hangover the next day ensured he went to work in a foul mood.

Muttering.

Snapping.

Refusing to tell anyone what happened.

Wendell sent him home. "Get out of here. I don't care if you had a fight with your girlfriend. We don't need you being a dick."

It was more than a fight. Much as he didn't want to believe it, she'd cheated on him. The woman he would have sworn was his mate. The one that made him ridiculously happy had betrayed him.

His apartment only depressed him further. Not only were there pieces of her scattered all over—like the underwear dangling from the corner of the bookcase—but Terror was still at her house.

He texted her about retrieving his cat, even as it might kill him to see her.

Her reply. *No.*

As if she could keep his pet. He was waiting at her house around the time she should come home. Only she didn't. He backtracked to the clinic to find it closed.

Where was she?

He knew where she hid the spare key in the yard. It wasn't hard to enter and discern his cat wasn't there, and neither was Honey.

Which led to panic. Had she been accosted on her way home?

He texted. *Where r u?*

She didn't reply.

He texted Dorian. *Do a locate on Honey's phone.*

It took only a few minutes for a reply. An eternity.

She's at her parents' place in the burbs.

So not dead. Good. Because a shattered heart didn't mean he wished her ill. Hell, if she'd been pregnant before they met, he would have gladly taken on the role of father. But the lie...

How could she betray him like that?

Thinking about it depressed him, so he hit a bar to get drunk. Completely wasted. Blasted out of his mind. So drunk he could barely walk by the time Dorian came to get him.

"What the fuck happened to you?" Dorian asked.

"She wasna da one," he slurred. It took a lot for

someone his size, and with his Lycan metabolism, to get incapacitated, but he managed it and kept it going. It took one full week of him calling in sick before Griffin showed up and barked, "What the fuck is wrong with you?"

"I is sad." His lips turned down. Ulric was especially sad because he'd run out of booze and had yet to locate his phone with the app to order more delivered.

"Dorian said something about you and some woman not working out."

"Not just any woman. Mine. She was supposed to be my mate. I felt it. In here." He thumped his chest. "She said she loved me. And then she just had to go and sleep with someone else."

"You caught her?"

"No." His lips turned down. "Never suspected it."

"Then what makes you so sure?"

He didn't have enough booze left in his system to ease the discomfort of this conversation. "She's pregnant." He spat the dirty word.

Griffin recoiled. "Oh." He paused. "You're sure it's not yours?"

That got his old friend a side-eye. "Duh, 'course it's not mine. You should know better than to even ask. Or have you forgotten the Pack pays the monthly bill to keep my swimmers on ice ever since I got the big snip?"

"And you're sure it's still intact?"

"I think I would have noticed if my vasectomy failed," was Ulric's sarcastic drawl.

"How?" Griffin asked. "Because, in most cases of recanalization occurring years after the procedure, the only real clue comes from accidental pregnancy."

Ulric blinked. "Hold on, are you saying my vasectomy might have healed itself?"

"While rare, it can happen."

"How the fuck have I never heard of this?" Ulric blurted out. Only to blanch. "Shit, does this mean there's a possibility I could be the daddy?" If that were true, then Honey hadn't lied and he was officially the biggest asshole in the world.

Griffin rolled his shoulders. "I'm only saying it's possible and something we should find out for sure. So let's get you tested. I'll speak to Maeve about collecting a sample and sending it off via her clinic."

Before Griffin even finished speaking, Ulric snapped his fingers. "We don't have to wait that long. We know someone who already has a sample and a lab."

Griffin couldn't talk him out of visiting Dr. Silver, but he did manage to convince Ulric to take a shower. He also shaved just in case he had to grovel later when begging Honey's forgiveness. Did anyone make a card that said, *Sorry I accused you of being a cheating whore?*

Fuck.

Dr. Silver took a few minutes to answer the door to her lab. She frowned at him. "You shouldn't be here. We're done testing."

"Testing is why I'm here. You have my jizz in a jar, so you'll know. Am I fertile?" he blurted out.

Her brows arched. "Excuse me?"

It took him only a moment to spill, "My girlfriend got pregnant and I accused her of cheating only Griffin says it's possible my vasectomy healed itself and so it turns out I might be the daddy and so I need my junk tested and since you already got a gob of my spunk I figured you'd know."

Her jaw dropped by the time he finished. "That was a lot of insanity in one giant run-on sentence."

"But you understand the problem. So, Doc, am I shooting blanks or swimmers?" He had yet to decide which he preferred. The one meant Honey'd betrayed him. The latter that he'd become a father who would now have to convince his mate to abort their child because otherwise the fetus would murder the mother. It was the one thing that had stuck to him when he'd been let in on the lycanthropy secret. He didn't understand the medical why's of it, just that something about the pregnancy proved fatal. Hence the snip. Hence why Honey couldn't be pregnant.

She couldn't die.

"I haven't actually gotten to that sample yet."

"Then what are we waiting for?" Ulric had no patience.

"It's frozen."

"I can give you a fresh cup," he offered.

She sighed. "You're going to pester me until I agree, aren't you?"

"Most likely."

"Fine. Grab a container and meet me in that corner." She pointed to an area with machines and test tubes strung in racks.

It took him longer than expected to spew. He'd think of Honey, get hard, then think of what he'd said and grow soft. By the time he came, he had convinced himself he was being an idiot. If he had live ones, wouldn't he know? Then again, the women he slept with insisted on condoms. He and Honey had progressed past that point.

He eventually exited with the goods in hand. If he expected Dr. Silver to be discreet about her handling of it, he got a shock. She slapped the container on a counter, got a swab, and dabbed it into the sample before smearing it on a slide.

"Ew," he couldn't help but mutter.

She glanced at him over her shoulder. "Seriously? It came from your body."

"It's not supposed to be played with."

"Hardly playing. Now do you want me to check for live swimmers or not?"

He slowly nodded. The moment of truth. The peek of revelation. The— What was taking her so long?

She jotted on a pad by her side.

"Well?" he exclaimed. "What's the verdict?"

"That depends. How do you handle bad news?

Because this lab has some very expensive stuff." The implication couldn't be clearer.

He swayed on his feet. "You're kidding, right?" he said faintly.

"I have it on solid authority that I lack a sense of humor. And while sarcastic, I am not a liar. There are definitely some live sperm in your sample, meaning you very likely got your partner pregnant."

"Oh fuck."

"In good news, by acting like an ass, she most likely doesn't want to keep the kid."

"She can't," he muttered. "It will kill her."

"Supposedly."

He glanced at her. "What's that supposed to mean?"

"That it's said, and yet I've yet to encounter anyone who's ever actually met someone who got preggers by a Lycan and died."

"Because no one wants to intentionally kill their mate and child." It seemed obvious to him.

"Yet mistakes happen. I'm looking at one right now."

He winced. "I didn't know it was possible after getting the snip."

"How could you not? It's part of the possible side effects they tell you about before doing the procedure."

"At the time, I was more concerned about how long before I could use it," he sheepishly admitted.

"Honestly, I'm surprised we haven't seen this

happen more often given the Lycan ability to heal. Your case makes a good point to introducing yearly testing to ensure we catch others."

"I can't believe this is happening," he groaned. "I accused her of cheating."

"Wow, that's rude."

"What else was I supposed to assume?"

Dr. Silver fixed him with a stare. "You should have assumed the woman you loved would never cheat on you and not been an asshole about it."

"But I didn't know."

"Is not an excuse. Better luck next time."

Next time? Honey had been his one and only chance.

Was there a way to salvage the situation? He couldn't find a card that said *Sorry for being a jerk*, so instead he brought flowers, chocolate, and an apology to her door.

A door she refused to open.

10

Honey didn't open the door to her place. She knew who stood on the other side. The man who broke her heart. She put a hand on her stomach. "It's okay, peanut. We won't let the big bad Viking inside."

"I heard that," he yelled.

Impossible. She'd barely whispered.

"I'm sorry, Honeybee. Can we talk?"

"No." A word spoken without crying. She'd shed enough of them at her parent's place.

"You can't ignore me forever. You're pregnant with my child."

That more than anything had her whipping open the door to offer him a glare. "Oh, so *now* it's your child? Ha. What happened to the great vasectomy?"

He looked sheepish as he said, "Apparently, my swimmers built a new tunnel. I'm not sterile after all."

"Well, good for you." She went to slam the door, but he wedged his foot inside.

"Can't we be adults and talk about this?"

"I was. You called me a whore and a liar."

He winced.

She opened the door, only to slam it on his foot. "Get. Out."

"But, Honey—" He was positively groveling. Contrite. Was she really the type to hold a grudge? He had, after all, had his sperm tested—because he felt bad or to further prove his conviction she must be a cheating slut?

"You may come in, but only to grab your box of things."

"Oh." His lips turned down.

She widened the door and stood back to point at the box she'd filled with all the random stuff he'd left lying around. More than she'd imagined in their short time. Each item a dagger to the heart.

Before he could bend and grab it, a furry dynamo came thumping down the stairs and leaped to say hello.

"Terror!" he exclaimed, beaming in pleasure as the kitten hung off the front of his shirt and meowed.

"You want him, take him." He'd been a right brat since Ulric left, as if punishing her for his absence. Not to mention seeing him was a constant reminder.

"I missed him." He chucked the kitten under the chin then eyed her. "I've missed you even more."

"Again, too late for apologies."

"Give me another chance. I swear I won't be an asshole."

She was tempted. She turned from him. "I don't think that's a good idea."

"Then will you at least listen? There are things you don't know about my genetics. Reasons why I had the vasectomy."

"History of hereditary disease?" Having seen it in the animals she treated, she knew all too well the dangers.

"In a sense. More like I have, um, tainted sperm."

She arched a brow. "Am I going to have a radioactive baby?"

He stammered. "No, not radioactive, but it is dangerous. You can't keep it."

"Not really your choice." She placed a hand on her belly.

"I am telling you this for your own good. That baby will kill you if you don't abort."

Her mouth rounded. "What is wrong with you? I won't get back together, so now you want to kill our child?"

"I don't want to. We have to."

"Get out." She lifted her arm and pointed.

"You have to listen to me, Honey. That thing in your uterus isn't normal."

"What's not normal is you. You don't want a child, I get it. I already told you I won't make you pay support. Heck, you don't even have to be on the birth certificate. But I am not murdering my baby just because you can't handle the responsibility."

"I am trying to save your life," he insisted.

"I don't need your help or advice. Goodbye, Ulric."

"But—"

"Don't make me call the cops."

Shoulders rounded and head bowed, he left.

She closed the door, locked it, then slumped, too mentally exhausted to cry.

For a moment, when he'd shown up ready to apologize, she thought maybe, just maybe, they could recover from this.

I couldn't have pegged it more wrong if I tried.

11

Ulric stalked from Honey's house, Terror clinging to his shoulder and hissing at the few people they passed. His kitten didn't leap until he entered the familiar main floor of Lanark Leaf. Ulric headed for the back and slumped in a chair.

Dorian whirled to eye him. "Wow, you look like shit."

"Thanks," he grumbled. "I've got a problem, and I don't know what to do."

"Wanna tell me about it? See if outside eyes can spot a solution?"

"Do you know a solution for the fact Honey got pregnant, I accused her of cheating, only to find out the snip failed, and she is carrying my child, which will kill her, but she refuses to even think about aborting and never wants to see me again?"

Dorian didn't blink the entire time. Just stared.

"Well?" Ulric asked.

"I think what you just said is probably why Doctor Silver popped in for a visit."

"She's here?"

"Upstairs with Griffin and Maeve—"

Ulric was moving before he'd finished speaking. He took the stairs two at a time, knocking when he reached the door at the top and standing impatiently, waiting to be let inside.

Maeve answered and smiled at him. "Ulric, come on in. Good timing. Griffin was just about to call you."

He strode in and saw Doctor Silver sitting at the kitchen island.

She didn't smile in greeting. Her expression remained blank. Not a good sign.

"I take it she ratted me out." He flung up his hands. "It's true, my super sperm rebuilt the canal to my dick. And as a result, Honey is pregnant."

No one congratulated him. Rather somber faces abounded all around. Except for Silver. She sipped her coffee without saying shit.

"So it is most definitely yours?" Griffin questioned.

"Yeah. Not that it matters in her mind. She won't talk to me. I went over to apologize and try to explain why she had to abort, and she tossed me out."

Maeve just about choked. "You told her to get rid of the baby?"

"Well, yeah. You know she can't keep it. It'll kill her."

"Not necessarily," Dr. Silver murmured.

He whirled to eye the doctor. "What's that supposed to mean?"

"Exactly what it sounds like. Under the right conditions, a fetus can survive."

"And the mother?"

"Sometimes."

He growled as he stalked closer. "What's that supposed to mean?"

"It means that there is a chance that both mother and child can survive the trauma of a Lycan pregnancy."

"You've seen this happen?"

"No. But a search of Cabal history records seems to indicate it used to be if not common, then not entirely unheard of."

"If it's possible, then why the rule we have to be neutered?"

"Because it's possible, not easy."

"What's involved?" Maeve asked. "Special dietary regime? Vitamins?"

"It doesn't matter," Griffin stated. "The rules are clear. Lycan pregnancies, even if accidental, must be terminated and the embryo destroyed. It's to protect our species. Disobedience on that point will draw the Cabal."

Who wouldn't hesitate to kill Honey to hide their existence. "How am I supposed to convince her when she won't even talk to me?" Ulric complained.

"What did you expect?" Maeve countered. "You told a woman, whom you love, who is happy to be pregnant with your child, that she has to kill it."

"Because I wanted to protect her," he countered.

"But from her perspective, think of how it looks," Maeve argued back.

"What else was I supposed to do?"

"In the past, slipping something into their food solved it. The mother thought she miscarried." The sly reply by the doctor had them all staring at her. Silver held her cup and uttered a flat, "What? This isn't the first time we've dealt with this exact type of scenario."

"Does this mean you're going to taint her food now that you know?" Ulric understood Honey couldn't keep the baby, but that didn't mean he was cool with her ingesting what amounted to poison.

"Actually, I've requested permission from the Cabal to try something else."

"Wait a second," Ulric interjected, "permission for what? What are you planning to do to Honey?"

"If the Cabal agrees, I plan to see if your former lover can carry the child to term."

"No."

"It's not your decision," Silver countered. "She's already stated she wants to keep it."

"Because she doesn't know any better, but you can go fuck yourself if you think I am going to sentence her to death to appease your morbid curiosity. You're talking about the woman I love."

"Very well, what's your plan then?" Silver asked. "Going to strap her down while someone forces an abortion on her? Slip the drugs into the food yourself?"

"If I can explain to her—"

"Explain what? That she's carrying a werewolf baby in her womb who might potentially tear her apart from the inside."

He cringed.

Griffin put a hand on his shoulder. "All this arguing is pointless until we know what the Cabal decides. If they say no, then we'll formulate a plan. Drugs to induce a miscarriage would be the easiest solution. Can we order those?" he asked of his wife.

Maeve winced. "Yes, but ethically you can't expect me to procure or administer them to her unknowingly. I love you, Griffin, and will do much to protect you and the pack, but I can't do that to someone, not with the oath I gave as a doctor to do no harm."

"And I would never ask you to." Griffin drew her close to his body.

"If anyone has to do it, it will be me," Ulric stated. He'd created this mess. He'd fix it.

"How about you all stick a pin in it and wait until the Cabal replies?" Silver said.

"How long for that?" Griffin asked.

"I should know by morning," Silver replied.

"And if they say yes, then what?" Ulric asked.

"Then we do everything in our power to help Honey Iris have a safe pregnancy."

"You've got to be fucking kidding me," Ulric muttered. "Wish I'd known this before I spun her some story about a fetal defect requiring an abortion. She hates me."

"She's your mate. Give her time," Griffin advised.

Easier said than done.

Honey refused to see him, speak to him, or have anything to do with him.

It had been a week since she'd kicked him out, days since the Cabal agreed with Silver's plan to monitor her pregnancy.

A week of lonely nights and regrets so he was understandably excited when she called him. Her voice soft and hushed as she whispered, "Help. I think someone's in my house."

12

Honey wasn't one to play games.
Usually.
And then she met Ulric.
Fell in love.
Got pregnant.
He turned into an ass.
He apologized.
Assed out again.
She stood up for herself and the baby.
Got lonely.
And scared.
What had he meant when he claimed there might be something wrong with the pregnancy? Was he being a lying jerk, or did she have to worry about something serious? She didn't have a family doctor since hers retired. The walk-in clinic and emergency weren't exactly the right places for a nervous expectant mother,

and yet she couldn't see a gynecologist without a referral. Freaking Canadian healthcare system had so many hoops to jump through. Sure she had access to an ultrasound with her practice, but would it show her if something was amiss?

What would she do if something affected the baby? Be brave like those who had children despite knowing they'd need extra care, or should she listen to Ulric and get an abortion? Both sounded scary. What if the baby was fine and Ulric lied? Being a mother sounded all good and exciting, but could she do this on her own? Her parents would offer to help, but they were in their sixties. Enjoying their golden years. It wouldn't be fair to them.

All these thoughts and more kept her company as she walked home from work. A prickle at her nape gave the sensation someone watched. A whirl to glance behind showed the sidewalk clear, and yet the feeling persisted.

Am I being stalked?

Was it Ulric? She'd not seen him and, given she'd blocked him, no longer got his texts. Would he resort to shadowing her? Having spent time with him she would have said he lacked the subtlety for spy work. If he lurked nearby, what could she do to flush him out? A sly idea to find out hit her.

She entered her house quickly, locking the door before jogging upstairs. Only then did she dial his number.

Right away he answered. "Honey."

She cut him off. "Help. I think someone's in my house."

"Oh fuck. Don't panic. Are you hiding?" he asked.

"Yes. In my closet." She kept whispering while watching out a window on the top floor.

"Good, stay there. I'm on my way."

"Where are you?"

"The shop. I'm working a late one on account Quinn's off."

"You've been there all day?" she confirmed as she saw someone exiting a car across the road. A tall guy wearing a ball cap and hoodie. He didn't walk like Ulric, but he headed for her side of the street.

"Yeah. So excuse me if I stink of weed. There was an incident with a new shipment and a cat who decided it was evil and took off with a package. Apparently, that little bugger is stronger than he looks. By the time I ripped it out of his mouth, shit was flying all over."

She almost smiled. She'd missed his stories. Missed him.

The tall man had crossed the road by now and headed for the corner of the street. Not Ulric after all. Although why park here and walk?

"I was mistaken. No one's here. You don't have to come over."

"I don't mind. I'm glad you called me."

She wandered from the bedroom toward the stairs.

"I don't know why I did. In a real emergency, you should be the last person I call."

"Yet I'd protect your life with my own."

"But not that of our child." She couldn't help the bitter retort.

He sighed. "If circumstances were different, you know I would love any child we created. That's not the issue. Your health and safety is."

"What if this medical issue that's got you so worried doesn't even present? You could be freaking for nothing. I haven't even seen a doctor yet."

"A doctor might not be able to diagnose it until it's too late."

"But shouldn't we at least try?" She slipped when she said we.

He caught it and said, "We could, but I'm scared for you, Bee. I don't want to lose you."

A phone wasn't the way to have this conversation. "Are you still coming over?"

"I'd like to."

"How far are you?"

"Just passing that place that sells the best Shawarma in Ottawa."

"Given Mr. Shawarma isn't anywhere close, that puts you pretty far."

"I miss this," he said suddenly.

She understood exactly what he meant. They'd had such a good repartee. While they didn't finish each other sentences, they'd meshed when it came to humor.

Could talk for hours or even just snuggle and watch a movie.

A pang hit her as she realized she'd called him not because she actually thought he stalked her but because she missed him. That feeling of being watched? Blame the pregnancy hormones.

She'd gone silent, and he queried with her name, "Honey?"

"Yeah."

"I'm at the end of your street."

"I'll let you in, but let me make one thing clear. This is only so you can tell me more. I haven't forgiven you," she stated, not just for his benefit. A part of her missed him so much. Wanted to understand because the Ulric she knew didn't jive with the one she'd met once she announced her pregnancy.

The Ulric she knew would have done backflips and insisted on carrying her around and holding her hair while she puked. The fact he reacted so strongly made her wonder if he'd been traumatized somehow in his past.

"I'll be a gentleman, I swear. I just want a chance to make things right."

"We'll see about that," she mumbled heading for the stairs to the main floor.

Thump. She paused mid-step and listened. Then said very softly, "Are you coming in through the back door?"

"No. Why?"

"I think someone's here. For real this time," she hissed as she heard a creak.

"Get your ass back in that closet. I'm almost there."

"The front door is locked," she stated, eyeing the remaining steps and the deadbolt.

"Don't you dare," he warned.

"I'm doing it," she huffed before leaping into action, pounding down the last few steps, throwing herself at the lock.

She never made it. Someone grabbed her hair and yanked. She shrieked.

Would have sworn she heard a dog howl.

She grabbed at the hands tangled in her hair, twisting and kicking. Whoever had a grip proved strong.

"Let go!" she demanded.

Instead, they punched her. The solid blow rocked her. She fell to her knees and wavered, blinking, her vision blurry. She heard the slam of her door forcefully opened and hitting the wall.

Then a seriously low growl like an animal. As she swayed to the side and hit the wall, she half turned to see Ulric had arrived. A hulking angry hunk of male who appeared rather feral as he stalked to her large assailant.

And she meant big.

The person who'd broken in and attacked her had his hair shaved short, a scar over his eye, and a sneer, and he had a few inches on Ulric. Not that it stopped her Viking. Possessed of a berserker rage, he went after the guy, ramming into his midsection and driving them hard into her kitchen island. Things rattled. Blows landed. She could hear the struggle going on while she sat on the floor. She struggled to fight the wooziness in her head and gain her feet.

The grunting and banging of a fight spurred her to stagger in the direction of her kitchen. Ulric. She had to help him. Entering, the first thing she saw was Ulric, his back to her facing—

She blinked. And blinked again. The wolf she hallucinated remained in her kitchen, snarling at Ulric. A dark beast with a scar over his eye, much like her attacker.

The two of them fought, the wolf snapping its jaws at Ulric while he tried to hold those teeth away from his flesh. It made no sense.

I think I have a concussion. She collapsed onto the floor, closing her eyes against the spinning and improbability of a wolf in her kitchen. She turned into a boneless heap with her cheek pillowed on the floor, eyes opening and closing slowly, giving her snapshots of the fight.

Ulric wrestling with the wolf.

The wolf biting his arm hard enough blood flowed.

Ulric baring his teeth and biting back!

Then his arms wrapped around the wolf's neck, and he hugged it tight before dropping to the floor.

Crack.

The wolf went limp.

He dropped the furry body and stood.

A true Viking, spattered in blood, who murmured, "You're safe, Bee."

She closed her eyes.

13

THE WOLF DIDN'T MOVE after Ulric snapped its neck. The limp body hit the floor, forever furry since he didn't change before death. A safety feature that helped keep their existence hidden.

Ulric rose to his feet as his gaze swung to find Honey. She lay slumped over on the floor. Fainted from shock, or had she succumbed to an injury given the rapidly blossoming bruise on her face?

"Fuck me." This was his fault. He'd arrived too late. Jogging when he should have been sprinting the second she called. He'd gotten caught up in the moment of connection. He'd had time to regret some of the things he'd said. He'd talked it over with Brandy, his closest female friend, and she'd pointed out some obvious facts he'd somehow missed.

For one, no man should ever tell a woman he impregnated to get an abortion unless he wanted to become a eunuch. As Brandy reminded him while poking him in the chest, "Her body, her choice."

"What if that choice kills her?" he'd argued.

"Which leads us to the second dumb thing you did. Telling her the pregnancy had to end because otherwise she'd die. What the hell is wrong with you?" Brandy had yelled. "That poor woman. She was probably all excited and a little bit scared to tell you—"

"She was," he murmured, remembering the shining uncertainty in her gaze.

"And you just wham, bam, slam her down not once but twice. You doubled down on being a douchebag."

The wince wasn't just because of Brandy's next slap. And before anyone thought she abused him, he'd been tickled harder in his life. He also deserved worse.

He'd acted abominably with Honey. Not putting himself in her position. She didn't know of Ulric's wolf heritage. Without that knowledge, he would have come across as cold and uncaring.

He hit the floor on his knees beside her. "Oh, Honey, I'm sorry." *For everything*.

This close he had no trouble discerning the steady pulse in her neck or the soft huffs of her breath. He didn't smell blood, but she could have internal injuries he didn't see. The bruise blossoming on her face had gotten dark quick.

While he wanted nothing more than to drag her into his arms and run—because a wolf in her house could only mean she'd been targeted—at the same time, the security specialist within kicked in. He had to secure the scene. Report what happened. Request backup and medical aid. The kind that wouldn't leave a trail for humans.

As he headed for the front door, he pulled out his phone and put out a general message to the Pack on their encrypted forum. Even then, he worded his request carefully.

A dog got into Honey's yard. Anyone wanna give me a hand corralling it? He hit Send as he reached the door. He shut and locked it without checking to see if anyone watched. At nine o'clock at night, though, they stood a good chance of being fine. Even if they weren't, too late to change anything now. He'd listen for wailing sirens.

He headed for the kitchen and called Griffin.

His boss answered. "What's going on? I just read the text." Griffin would have ensured the line was scrambled even before answering. Declan had them all outfitted with the latest tech, but that didn't mean Ulric fully trusted it. Not too long ago, they'd had a spy listening in on them.

"Glad you're up. I need a hand with a rabid dog." Code for "Lycan situation."

"What makes you think it's rabid?"

"No moon and yet I could swear I see crazy in its eyes."

Griffin sucked in a breath as he caught the

message: A wolf shifted without the moon and attacked. "Is Honey okay?"

It killed Ulric to see her on the floor. He wanted to scream, *"No she's fucking not,"* but he had to stay cool. "Well, she's not too impressed by the mess she made when the fucker scared her. Which reminds me, bring some garbage bags. Maybe some bleach. Pasta will come out of grout, right?"

That cryptic message told Griffin they had a body situation with blood.

"There goes my Friday night with my wife." Griffin kept playing along even as he probably had questions.

"Speaking of wife, you should bring Maeve to keep Honey company." She'd still yet to move or make a sound.

"Coming. I'll bring Quinn too. He's got a way with wild animals."

Ulric hung up, tension making his muscles taut despite the cavalry on its way. He stood between Honey and the wolf, torn between removing the body before she woke and doing something—fucking anything—for her. But he was no doctor. He couldn't even be sure if moving her wouldn't do more damage. Didn't paramedics and 911 always tell people to not move victims? He clenched his fists because that went against his urge to gather her close and lend her his strength.

Maeve would be here shortly. Griffin wouldn't

fuck around. What Ulric should do was perhaps gather some clues as to why this fucker had attacked Honey in the first place. That couldn't be a coincidence.

Ulric had the door open for Griffin and Maeve before they even knocked.

The doctor's gaze went immediately to Honey. She didn't even remove her coat or shoes as she strode briskly to Honey's side. "What happened?"

"Not entirely sure. By the time I broke in, Honey was weaving on her feet. I think the bastard who broke in hit her."

Maeve knelt by her side. "Definite contusion on the left side of her face. She'll have a shiner for sure. Nose doesn't appear broken, though."

"So she's okay?" He couldn't hide the worry in his tone.

"Hard to tell until I examine her further."

"I didn't move her," he hastened to say.

"Good, let's see if anything's broken." Maeve quickly ran a visual inspection before shifting Honey to further check for damage, muttering, "Everything looks intact, but she most likely has a concussion given the shiner she's going to wake up with."

"What about the baby?"

"I can't tell with what I have here. We should take her to my clinic for a more thorough exam."

"Before you steal Ulric, a few questions, such as what the fuck happened? And who is that?" Griffin asked, pointing to the wolf.

"Don't know who. He broke into Honey's house. I was chatting with her while on my way over when I heard her scream. I kind of lost it after that," Ulric admitted, hanging his head.

Griffin clapped him on the back. "Can't say as I blame you. We'll talk more shortly. Get Honey to the clinic. Use my car." A timely offer given Ulric's was too far. He'd been walking to work, needing the exertion to tire out his mind.

"Ulric"—Maeve pointed to Honey—"can you carry her out?"

Given he'd waited for permission, he wasted no time scooping Honey up, gently rising with her. As he did, Maeve kissed Griffin while taking his keys.

She'd accepted Griffin as he was. Could he ever expect the same with Honey? How could he even explain what happened tonight?

Griffin's car was parked right out front. For that short stint, Ulric made it seem like Honey walked by his side, even as his arm kept her upright. Maeve flanked her, pretending gaiety, a group of friends going out.

They slid Honey into the backseat, where Ulric held her on the short ride to the clinic. Once there, he carried her in, seeing as how Dorian could access and control the feeds of all the cameras in the alley. In other words, no one would be watching that shouldn't.

Maeve flicked on lights as she dropped her purse

and shrugged off her coat. "Take her into exam room two."

As he stepped into the space, he faltered. To his surprise, Dr. Silver was there. "Why are you here? Did Griffin call you?"

"I did," Maeve declared, entering behind him. "While I'm good at diagnosing and fixing a bunch of medical issues, Dr. Silver is more knowledgeable about the child Honey's carrying."

"She was punched," Silver noted as he lay Honey on the medical bed.

"Yeah. But I don't know what else might have happened before I got there."

Maeve began examining Honey thoroughly, shining a light in her eyes, taking her pulse. Silver was just as busy, fitting a blood pressure cuff and palpating limbs.

"Nothing visibly broken," Silver announced.

"Heart rate is normal. Flesh is responsive. I expect she'll waken shortly with a hell of a headache."

Ulric didn't say it, but Silver did. "No sign of a miscarriage, but no idea if any trauma was done to the baby until we get a peek inside."

"Did you bring the portable ultrasound machine?" Maeve asked.

Silver nodded and rolled over a trolley with a small machine sitting atop, a wand on a cord coiled in front of it.

"Nice setup. I've been thinking of getting one for

the clinic." Maeve appeared very interested in the tech while Ulric wondered what they'd see inside Honey's belly.

Turned out the thing that might kill her really was a baby. A baby he'd told her to abort. A baby that took shape with a head, two arms, two legs. Until that moment, the pregnancy had been a concept. Easy to dismiss for him because he had no attachment. Honey got it the moment it began growing in her belly, and it hit him as he saw the little person taking shape on the screen, a person that he'd help make.

"How do we stop the child from killing her?" he asked softly of Silver.

"I have a few ideas, but they will require her cooperation," the doctor said point-blankly.

"Like?"

"Like the fact she'll have to be taken somewhere she can be monitored twenty-four-seven. We'll be testing her and tracking the growth of the fetus."

"You're going to lock her up and make her a science experiment?" He saw through the words to the gist.

"We don't have much choice. She's carrying a Lycan child. You know a human doctor won't know how to help her when she runs into trouble."

"Maybe she won't?" He couldn't help a hopeful lilt.

"She will, and that's why she needs me."

"You sound as if you have a plan."

"I do."

"How can you know it will work if you've never encountered a Lycan pregnancy before?"

"I don't know, but I'll tell you one thing; without me, she dies for sure."

"She is going to hate me," he muttered.

"You should try telling her the truth," Maeve murmured. "Griffin had that same fear. He thought I wouldn't accept him if I knew."

"One big difference, you and Griffin were totally in love by the time he told you."

"And you aren't?"

"I am, but I don't know how Honey feels about me anymore." He'd made so many mistakes.

"Then what do you have to lose? Tell her the truth," Maeve suggested.

"I'm supposed to get permission from the alpha for that."

Maeve gave him a look as she said, "Are you telling me to go ask my husband's permission?"

"No?" Ulric had once more blundered.

Maeve laughed. "Maybe you're not that dumb after all."

"Don't count on it," Silver retorted, leaving the room first. Maeve followed and left Ulric alone with Honey.

He sat in a chair while Honey slept. He'd been told to not wake her, which went contrary to everything he knew about head wounds. Apparently, the science of it changed.

He dozed on and off, waking at the slightest creak, which usually turned out to be Silver checking on Honey's vitals every few hours.

He caught himself drooling when he woke at the muffled rumble of a man's voice. He emerged from the exam room to see Griffin arriving with Maeve, the former carrying a tray of coffees while Maeve held the box of pastries.

"Coffee?" Griffin handed over a supersized cardboard cup.

"Hell yeah." Ulric chugged half before sighing.

"Long night?"

"Hard to sleep not knowing if she's gonna wake. Not to mention I kept worrying another fucker was going to come for her."

"Isn't love grand?" Griffin riposted as his wife wandered off to check on Honey.

"I thought this whole love thing was supposed to make me feel good," Ulric grumbled, taking another sip of his coffee.

"It does when shit's going well. It's terrifying when it's not."

"Enough with the feelings crap. What happened to the body?"

"Quinn and I bagged the wolf and dumped it in the woods," Griffin recounted.

"Did you find any identifiers?" he asked.

Griffin shook his head. "The scraps of clothes were

generic. No wallet. No keys. Nothing. Not even a phone. What about you? Remember any details about the guy?"

"I barely looked at him," Ulric admitted even as he replayed the fight. The guy had shaggy brown hair, big, beetled brows, and— "He had a scar through here." He slashed over his eyebrow.

"Which isn't much to go on." Griffin sighed. "I'm hoping Dorian will get a hit from the DNA and fingerprints."

"And if he doesn't, then what?"

Griffin shrugged. "Not sure."

"He was Lycan."

"Obviously, but we don't know where he came from."

"Don't we?" Ulric's shoulders rolled forward. "This is my fault."

"We don't know that for sure."

A disparaging noise left him. "What are the chances it's not, though?"

"Good thing you were on your way over when it happened. You guys' patching things up?" Griffin asked.

"Doubtful. Did you know Silver wants to basically lock her up in a tower until the baby comes?"

"Silver wants to keep her alive."

"No, I want to keep Honey alive. Silver wants to study her and try out some theories. But what if those theories are wrong? What if..." Ulric couldn't say it.

"If you're really that worried, we could do it now. I know a guy who can get us the drugs."

Ulric blinked at him. "Force an abortion?" She'd never forgive him for as long as she lived. And then there was the fact a real baby grew inside her. His child.

Could he forgive himself?

"Well?" Griffin prodded. "It's up to you."

Ulric shook his head. "No. This isn't my call to make. It's hers, but only if she knows the truth. All of it. Then she can decide what she wants to do. I just need your permission." While Maeve had claimed Ulric could, he wanted to be sure.

"I think in this situation it's warranted," Griffin stated.

"Even if it puts us at risk?"

"We already are at risk. Someone attacked Honey. A Lycan who went through some trouble to be untraceable. I can't think of too many reasons to do that."

Ulric could, though, and he blurted out, "Could it be the Cabal?" They knew about Honey and her pregnancy, yet Silver said they'd given permission for the pregnancy to go forth.

Griffin appeared grave as he muttered, "I'd like to say no, but then again, I hate coincidences. At the same time, doesn't matter who it was, I guess. If she was targeted, they might try again."

"How am I supposed to keep her safe?"

"By taking her into hiding while the rest of us try and figure it out," Griffin stated.

"And by hiding you mean take her to whatever prison Silver has planned. Is that wise? Silver works for the Cabal. If they're behind it…"

"Why would they attack when they gave Dr. Silver the option to follow through with the pregnancy in the first place?" Griffin countered.

"I guess. And not really my biggest problem." His lips turned down. "Fuck me. Honey's never going to believe me."

"The full moon is in a few days," Griffin reminded him. "You can show her the proof then."

"Oh, because shifting in front of her will so make things right." Ulric grimaced. "It's like the world wants her to hate me."

He left Griffin and hit the bathroom for a quick splash of water to the face before returning to Honey. During that short time he'd left room was, of course, when she chose to wake up.

14

A STRANGE SMELL first alerted Honey to the fact she wasn't lying in her bed. A blink of her eyes showed a ceiling overhead, the tiles definitely not familiar.

"And she finally wakes," drawled a feminine voice.

A turn of Honey's head showed a woman sitting on a stool, half turned from the laptop on the counter. Her short, spiked hair, the tips of it light, highlighted a face with a pointed chin.

"Where am I? Who are you?" Honey pushed herself up on her elbows.

"I'm Dr. Silver. You're currently being treated at a small clinic. You suffered a blow to the head during a home invasion."

Her fingers went to her throbbing temple. "I was attacked!" The memory flooded over her. The terror as she'd been grabbed. The pain of the blow. A blurry recollection of Ulric bursting into her house and coming to her rescue.

And then things got strange because she recalled him wrestling with a wolf.

The lady kept talking. "You were assaulted last night. You'll notice half your face is a lovely color this morning, but good news, no permanent damage."

A relief. "How did I get here?"

"Ulric brought you. He knows the woman who runs this clinic." Dr. Silver didn't ask before she aimed a penlight into her eyes.

"Do you mind?" Honey turned her head, unable to quell her crankiness.

"Well, you're certainly coherent. Definitely not listless. Other than your head, how is the rest of you feeling?"

"Fine. But I'm pregnant." Her hand went to her flat belly.

"The fetus is fine. For now."

An ominous phrase to use. "What's that supposed to mean? Is there something wrong?"

"Maybe. We'll know more after we run some tests."

"Who's this we? I haven't agreed to anything, nor am I sure I want you as my physician." The bedside manner of this lady really lacked.

"I'm afraid you don't have much of a choice."

"What's that supposed to mean?" Honey pushed herself into a proper seated position and swung her legs over the edge of the bed.

"Ask Ulric," the doctor said just as he entered, the edges of his hair and face damp, his eyes wide.

"You're awake!" He sounded relieved.

"Kind of wishing I wasn't given what I woke to." She couldn't help her sour tone. It matched her throbbing head and mouth.

"Are you okay?" he hastened to ask.

"Not really. This woman thinks she can just declare herself my doctor. I've got news for you. No." Honey glared.

"Then I'd suggest getting an abortion sooner rather than later."

The bluntness of the woman shocked. "Excuse me? I don't think so. Did you put her up to this?" she accused Ulric.

Before he could reply, Dr. Silver snorted. "The only thing this idiot did was trust a vasectomy and try to keep you alive by giving you good advice. Which you've repeatedly rejected. But here's the thing. Without me as your doctor, you will die, along with that baby. So do as you want. Be stubborn or accept the help I'm offering. Up to you." Dr. Silver shrugged.

"I'm going to stick to a doctor I trust," Honey huffed. She went to hop off the bed, and Ulric was there to catch her. Good thing since she stumbled. She ended up against him. "Can you take me home?"

"Your home has been compromised." Dr. Silver would not shut up.

Honey whirling and snarled, "I wasn't talking to

you." Then more softly, "Please, Ulric, I just want my bed."

The torn expression on his face pitted her stomach.

"I'm sorry, Honeybee, I really am. But we have to do as Dr. Silver says."

She pushed away from him. "No, I don't."

"You have to understand. I'm doing this to help you and our baby."

"Since when is it *our* baby?"

"If you're going to insist on keeping it, then I'm going to do everything I can to ensure you're safe. And that means you need to listen to Dr. Silver. She truly is the only person who can help."

Honey shook her head. "I don't understand. This isn't how healthcare works. I'm the patient. I get to choose who is in charge of my care, not you, and most certainly not her." Another glare wasted on Dr. Silver, who appeared to be packing a medical bag.

The doctor addressed her next statement to Ulric. "Better talk fast. We leave soon. Oh, and don't even think of running with her. I can only do so much to protect you." With that, Dr. Silver left, and Honey unloaded.

"What's she talking about? Why this interest in my pregnancy? Is this some kind of black-market stuff involving the sale of babies?" Blame the accusation on a rabbit hole she'd followed one night after an episode about it on some crime show.

"No. We would never. I would never…"

"Then what is this about? Because I'm really fucking confused." She used a vulgar word that matched her mood.

"It's complicated."

"Then explain."

"You won't believe me."

"Try." Because at this point any kind of explanation would be welcome.

"I'm not like other men."

"Obviously. You're like inches above the average."

"It goes further than that. I'm, uh..." He hesitated before saying, "special."

"Given the number of stupid things you've said, not surprised."

"Not that kind of special. I'm a Lycan."

She stared at him.

He shifted uncomfortably. "Aren't you going to say something?"

"No, because I'm waiting for the truth."

"I told you, I'm a Lycan. You know, a werewolf."

"I heard you the first time and am not amused."

"This isn't a joke. It's the whole reason why I got the vasectomy. Werewolves can't have babies. Something about the change makes pregnancy fatal to the mother and child."

She eyed his serious mien before blurting out, "Oh my god, you actually believe that."

"Because it's true. I am a werewolf."

Laughter bubbled out of her. "That is the most inane thing I've ever heard."

"How is it inane? I know you saw that guy turn into a wolf just last night."

She waved a hand. "A hallucination brought on by my head injury." Never mind the fact he shouldn't have known what she'd seen.

"It wasn't a dream or some dazed vision. That guy who attacked you was a Lycan. The thing I don't know is why he went after you. Is it because we're mates, because you're pregnant, or was it just random?"

"You're crazy," she murmured. How had she not seen it? It explained so much, like his infatuation with her.

Ulric huffed and eyed the ceiling. "No, I'm not."

"If you're a werewolf, then prove it." She crossed her arms and waited.

"I can't."

"Because werewolves aren't real."

"Because I need a full moon."

"When's the next one?"

"In three days. Are you hungry?" He tried to change the subject.

"Starved. But I have waffles in the freezer at home. You're not invited." So much for making up. She couldn't date a crazy man.

"You can't go home. It might not be safe."

"Excuse me, but where else should I go? Your place, I assume?"

"Nope. Not safe either, which is why we're going to a safe house."

"No I'm not."

"Yeah you are."

"I'd like to see you try." Her gaze narrowed on him.

He flinched. "I'll be right back."

He left, but she was on his heels and emerged to see Dr. Silver speaking to a woman with dark hair bound in a bun, wearing a white coat.

Despite a lack of shoes, Honey went marching for the door. Ulric caught her around the waist, and she snapped.

"Let me go!"

"I can't, Bee. I'm sorry. This really is for your own good." He apologized even as she wriggled and kicked. It made no difference. He held her while Dr. Silver poked her with a needle.

When she woke, it was to find herself a prisoner.

15

A SHIT SITUATION GOT WORSE. Not only did Honey not believe him when he tried to tell her the truth, he'd had to manhandle her while Dr. Silver put her to sleep.

As he held a limp Honey in his arms, his heart broke. How could he mend this with his mate? It seemed like fate conspired against him.

Dr. Silver didn't suffer the same angst, although Maeve did chew her lower lip. "Maybe I should have talked to her. It must have been a lot to take in."

"This is my fault she's in this situation." Ulric never was one to shy away from hard things. Griffin claimed it was one of the reasons he asked him to become part of their Pack.

Dr. Silver—she of no moral compass—shook her keys. "You can play who's the most to blame later. We need to move her while she's sedated. My van is parked in the alley. I'll drive."

He didn't argue since it put him in the back with Honey. He sat with her head cradled in his lap and resisted the urge to sigh melodramatically. He'd waited all his life to find the one, and he'd borked it royally. Was there any way of coming back from his?

"Where are we going?" he asked rather than dwell on his failures.

"Secluded property about two hours outside of town."

"Her parents are going to notice she's gone missing."

"Not if her boyfriend whisked her off for an impromptu holiday before the pregnancy advanced too far." Silver had a ready reply.

"A boyfriend they've never even met? That won't get the cops called at all." He rolled his eyes.

"I guess you didn't see the TikTok Honey posted. It showed the departure board in the airport for Cancun, Mexico, and then the front of a brochure for a cruise."

"How the fuck did you manage that?"

"Some of us weren't being melodramatic."

He flattened his lips. "Her parents will still expect a call."

"She can call when we know she won't tell secrets."

"You can't be serious!" he exclaimed.

"You know we have to be careful. Hopefully Honey will see rationale quickly."

He had his doubts, and they didn't improve on the

drive. "What can you tell me about where we're going?"

"It belongs to a hockey player. He only rarely uses it in the summer during his off season, but it's actually equipped to work year-round and is rented when he's working for his team. It's got five bedrooms, three bathrooms, a great room, and acres of land, the perimeter of it under surveillance."

That didn't do justice to the giant log home they drove up to. Massive logs, which would likely get a company in trouble for cutting them today, framed the original front with its grand doors and peaked roof. To either side, flanked stone additions, the river stone partially covered by drying ivy, as the leaves turned brittle before the approach of winter.

A paddock attached to a barn to the left, a massive garage to the right. A gigantic pond. Woods.

It was... "Paradise." He uttered it aloud, and for once, Silver didn't sound stuffy or dry as she agreed.

"It is."

The question being, would Honey think so as well?

Entering the house, he noticed the sprawling peaked ceiling with its massive bank of windows framing the back. The view of a lake rivetted. He carried Honey with him as he approached the glass. The house had been built about two feet from a steep decline, zigzagged with a staircase that led to the rocky shore of a lake.

A kitchen opened to the left of the great room.

"Three of the bedrooms are upstairs. Master and bedroom slash den on this floor."

"Which one is Honey's?"

"Master. It's got the best security."

He carried her into a massive space to the right of the kitchen. It could have fit several beds. It held a king, a fireplace with flanking chairs, a jet tub in a corner, and a bathroom to make even him jealous.

He lay her atop the covers, wondering when she'd wake. He held her hand tucked in his, head bowed, wondering what he'd say.

Maybe there wasn't anything to say until he showed her. Once she realized he spoke the truth about being a Lycan, then maybe she'd truly listen to everything else he had to say.

She stirred, and he lifted his head to find her staring at him, expression soft at first then hardening into annoyance. He didn't expect the punch to his nose.

16

Honey hit Ulric. She, a usually non-violent person who literally carried spiders outside, punched the father of her child in the face.

It hurt her knuckles, but it also felt glorious.

He recoiled.

She wasn't done. "You bastard!" She remembered him holding her as that bitch doctor poked her with a needle.

Ulric held up his hands in a conciliatory gesture. "I'm sorry. I had no choice."

"You kidnapped me!" she accused.

"Because it literally meant the difference between life or death."

"Do you say that to all the girls? How many others have you abducted, you sick pervert?" Disdain unleashed, she pushed herself off the massive bed. Her feet hit the plushest carpet to ever spoil her tootsies. A glance down showed her feet sunken in the softness, the very light beige strands unmarred by stains, pet hair, or a single crumb. It appeared as immaculate as the massive room around her, replete with a gigantic bed made of actual logs. They matched the nightstands and dresser of knotted wood. A fireplace of stone with a mantel hung with a television faced the bed. A pair of chairs sat in front of it. Another set angled for a perfect view out of a huge window, which, even from here, showed a splendid panorama of forest and water.

Ulric interrupted her contemplation of the room. "It's not abduction but rather an intervention."

Her gaze narrowed. "It's like you want me to hit you again." Her fist clenched.

"I can explain everything now that we're here."

"Where exactly is here? Whose house is this?" Because the luxury around her boggled the mind.

"It's a rental. But no worries. it can't be traced back to us. It's the perfect hiding place."

She latched on the latter part. "Hiding from who?"

"Whoever sent that guy to your house."

"Why would someone have sent him?" She didn't follow his logic, not exactly surprising given it came from the guy who thought himself a werewolf.

"It's possible he went after you because of the baby. But Billy says I should keep an open mind in case it's actually something else."

"Who's Billy?"

"A member of our Pack and a cop. Detective as a matter of fact."

"And does this detective look the other way when girls go missing around you?"

He had the nerve to sigh. "You're overreacting. You'll understand everything once I explain."

"Got another story for me? Going to ditch the werewolf persona and become what, vampire next?"

"This is serious, Honey. Someone came after you. They might try again."

"And you think it's because of the bun in my oven." She placed a hand on her stomach. "Why would anyone care if I'm pregnant?" It hit her in a flash. "Wait a second... Are you married or something? Am I being targeted by your crazy-ass wife?"

"What? No!" He couldn't have looked more horrified if he tried.

"Girlfriend?"

"No."

"Do you owe someone money? Were they going to ransom me?"

"No."

"But this is somehow your fault, isn't it?"

"Given the man who attacked was Lycan, it's a possibility."

"Oh my god, would you stop it with the whole werewolf schtick. Come on. I'm not an idiot. I'm not into cosplay or whatever it is you're doing."

"It's the truth, and I'll prove it two nights from now."

"You going to change into a wolf and howl at the moon?" she taunted.

"Yep." Spoken quite seriously.

A more gullible woman would have believed him. "I don't know how I didn't see the crazy before," she claimed with a shake of her head.

"You'll see it's true soon enough, and then we can talk rationally about the situation."

"Is that when I should expect your next abortion push?" Which she'd admittedly thought of. Being told the pregnancy might kill her had that effect, not to mention she'd always imagined having a child with someone she loved and who would be there as not only a father to the child but a lover and best friend to her. Boy had she misjudged Ulric.

"I learned my lesson. I won't tell you what to do."

"What he is going to do is allow you to make an informed choice." Dr. Silver entered, and Honey literally growled. Maybe Ulric's madness was contagious.

"You drugged me," Honey accused, jabbing a finger in her direction.

"I did."

"You might have hurt my baby."

"I'm a doctor, not an idiot. The baby is fine. You, on the other hand, might not be. Ulric wasn't lying when he said you could die. Most likely horribly if old accounts are to be believed."

"No real doctor would ever say to that someone. You're both crazy. Who came up with this sick game? What is this like extreme LARPing werewolf style? Are you getting a sick kick out of terrorizing a pregnant woman?"

"You hardly look terrified," the so-called doctor replied dryly. "What you are is stubborn and quite frankly more stupid than I would have expected from someone in your field. Do I look like a person who likes to role play for amusement?"

Her lips turned down. "I don't know what kind of person you are."

"In two days, you'll see your oversized sperm donor is telling the truth."

"Ew." Honey wrinkled her nose.

So did Ulric. "That was uncalled for."

Dr. Silver shrugged. "But truthful. I have better things to do than argue with someone being so willfully ignorant. I'll be back shortly to take your vitals."

"Like fuck you will," Honey grumbled.

"So you don't want me to check on the baby?"

Honey wanted more than anything to know what was happening inside her body, but the doctor was right about one thing. She could be stubborn, and she wasn't cooperating with her kidnappers. "I don't want you anywhere near me or my child."

"Very well. I'll return when you come to your senses. Let's go." The doctor snapped her fingers at Ulric.

He glanced at her. "I am not your dog to order around."

"Actually, if you want me to stick around to help her, then, yes, yes you are. I have better things to do than deal with this." She waved a hand at Honey.

"You can't leave. She needs your help."

"Then you'll do as I say." The doctor waited in the doorway.

Ulric appeared torn. Honey made the decision easy for him.

"Get out. I don't want to see you either."

"Honeybee, I'm—"

"Don't you dare apologize. I won't forgive you for this, Ulric."

His shoulders rounded, and he sighed. "Holler if you need anything."

"How about my freedom?" she spat.

"Are you always this melodramatic, or is it the hormones?" Dr. Silver dryly asked.

"Argh!" Honey grabbed the nearest thing, which happened to be a knickknack on the dresser, and threw it.

The doctor easily sidestepped and tsked. "Your aim is terrible." With that, she left.

Ulric hesitated.

"Get. Out."

He left, and the door shut behind him.

She never heard it lock, but when she tried the

handle, it didn't open, and a pad beside the door kept asking for validation.

"Argh!" She slapped her hands on the thick wooden panel before turning to pace while muttering, "I can't believe they did this." The pair of them working in cahoots because he didn't want to be a dad. It was working. Did she really want to be tied for life to a guy who would condone her kidnapping and try to make her believe he was a werewolf? Why couldn't he be like a normal fellow and just ghost her? This seemed so elaborate.

The only thing she couldn't complain about? The accommodations. She was a prisoner in the most luxurious room she'd ever seen, with a decadent bathroom, featuring a tub deep enough to soak with jets. Not that she stripped to try it. It seemed wrong to decry foul play while basking in a hot bubble bath.

The view from the windows showed her in some kind of rural location with an epic view of a spreading forest and a dark blue lake. Paradise if she wasn't a prisoner.

A knock at the door preceded it opening to reveal Ulric bearing a tray and, racing in through his feet, Terror.

"I'm not hungry." She turned her back to him.

"Don't do that. I know you are. You haven't eaten all day."

"And who's fault is that?" she snapped.

"You know what," he hotly retorted right back, "I'm doing the best I can in a shit situation."

"Also your fault. I wish I'd never met you," she lied. Because ignore the time since she peed on a stick, and before that she'd truly never been happier. Even now, with him being crazy, she missed him.

"We were fated to meet, Bee. And soon you'll understand why. You'll see why I've been so secretive."

She snorted. "I believe you're a werewolf like I believe aliens live amongst us."

"They probably do. Although I've never met anyone who smelled alien."

"I like the way you keep slipping those tiny werewolf bits in."

"Two more days and I'll show you."

The longest two ever, which included pacing that room, refusing Dr. Silver's offers for examination, rebuffing Ulric's attempt at reconciliation, wanting to protest by ignoring the trays of food, and failing because she was just so damned hungry. Even the nausea couldn't put her off.

By now someone had to have noticed her disappearance. Francis or her parents. Surely the cops were already searching for her. At the same time, as Honey wondered about a possible rescue, she had to admit, despite being a prisoner, she wasn't being abused in any way.

The food was excellent and plentiful, her accommodations more than adequate. Entertainment was provided in the form of television, books, and games. Cuddles with the kitten. She just wasn't allowed to leave or call anyone.

On the day of the full moon, Dr. Silver arrived after dinner, just before twilight.

"How are you feeling?" she asked.

"Fine." Not entirely true. Honey had felt jittery all day.

"You don't seem fine."

"Would you? Tonight, my boyfriend is determined to prove to me he's a lunatic."

"According to you. But what if you're wrong? What if he does shift, what then? Will you be able to handle it, or will your fragile mind collapse under the weighted realization that the world is vaster than you expected and you are less informed than you snottily like to admit."

At times, given how hard they pushed the narrative, Honey almost believed them. "Why are you helping him?" she asked instead.

"I'm helping you. He has nothing to do with this."

"He's the reason why I'm pregnant."

"But you're the one who will have to fight to survive." Dr. Silver glanced at her watch. "It's getting close to time. Are you ready to apologize for being a twat?"

"We'll see who's apologizing," she mumbled as they headed for the window.

She stood with her arms crossed, watching as Ulric

emerged from the house. He wore no shirt, just some low-riding track pants. Seeing him half-dressed brought a flushed reminder of previous times she'd admired his body.

"He's in good shape," Dr. Silver remarked, and Honey had to ball her fists lest she punch the doctor for looking at her man.

Because, despite it all, Honey still craved Ulric. Wanted him so badly it hurt.

He glanced at the window and caught her eye. He said nothing. Just stood there, waiting. It had to be chilly, given that in late November it went below zero at night.

The cloudy skies remained thick. His head turned to it as if waiting. A rift formed in the gray layer, and a beam of moonlight struck his upturned face. His hands went to the waistband of his pants, and he shoved them down, momentarily naked in the moonlight.

He started changing right away. His body contorted, the flesh changing as fur sprouted. Hands turned to paws. Face to muzzle. Until a golden-brown wolf stood there, staring at her with Ulric's eyes.

He told the truth. The shock of it kept her silent, even as Dr. Silver muttered a triumphant snickered, "Now do you believe?"

The wolf lifted its head and uttered a howl. Her stomach clenched.

I'm pregnant with a werewolf's baby.

The clouds further parted, spreading the moonlight, the glow of it hitting her in the window.

The sudden cramp in her midsection had her gasping. The sharp pain came again, and she couldn't help but cry out as she slumped.

The last thing she heard was Dr. Silver barking, "Get her to the wine cellar."

17

The next morning...

"What happened? Is she okay?" A frantic Ulric charged naked into the house. Because he wasn't an alpha who could change at will, he'd waited all night to shift back into skin so he could express his panic in something other than mournful howls. Paws meant he couldn't open the door to see why Honey screamed in pain.

Quinn did emerge at one point to tell him, "Go for a run and calm down. Your mate is fine for the moment."

The run didn't help. He couldn't help reliving that moment she'd stared as he shifted. Then the fact she'd cried out and crumpled. Overcome with shock at his change, or was it something else?

Junk dangling, Ulric sprinted barefoot for the

master bedroom, only to be stopped by a drawled, "Might want to put some pants on first."

He turned to see Quinn sitting on a stool by the kitchen island, eating some toast while Terror did his best to try and stick his head in the glass of orange juice. The jerk had avoided shifting the previous night. He'd been close to Ulric's mate. The smell on his clothes didn't lie.

A bristling Ulric swaggered up to the other male to growl, "Why did you touch her?"

"Relax. I only carried her to the cellar on the doctor's orders."

"What happened? Is Honey okay?"

"Doc says she seems fine. But she's gonna keep her downstairs a while longer just in case."

"What do you mean downstairs? What the fuck is going on?"

"Your woman had a reaction to moonlight."

"Not her, the baby. Oh fuck. I need pants." Ulric dashed to the den holding his bag of clothes, practically jumping into a shirt and bottoms before bolting back into the kitchen, where he growled at Quinn, "Where's the basement door?"

"By the mudroom at the back."

He found the door and took the steps down into an old stone-block cellar. The ceiling was low, especially in spots with running ductwork for the propane furnace. A newer wall closed an area, and from behind the door, he heard the murmur of voices. Before he could enter, Dr. Silver emerged.

She pursed her lips. "About time you stopped howling."

"Is Honey okay?"

"She seems stable for the moment."

"What happened?" he asked, hoping Quinn misunderstood.

"It's a Lycan baby, and it was a full moon. I think it tried to shift."

"That makes no sense. The baby hasn't been born, hence its skin wasn't exposed to the rays." Because it took the moon's touch to give the wolf the extra oomph it needed to come out.

"It would seem its mother can act as a conduit."

A chill went through him. "How is that possible? She's not Lycan, and technically neither is the child. I thought only the bite could turn us."

"That we know of. Until I can test the baby's DNA, we won't know for sure."

"But you expected it," he remarked, eyeing the wall. "You had this built."

"No, the cold cellar already existed. But I theorized this might happen, so I ensured we had a location that offered thick insulation and no windows."

"You blocked her from moonlight."

"Yes. As soon as we removed the exposure, she stabilized. I'll do an ultrasound later when she moves back upstairs. She's sleeping right now on the cot Quinn set up."

A cot? "When can I take her upstairs?"

"Soon. I'd like to give her a chance to rest before we risk relocating her. Keep in mind, while we moved quickly, she still suffered a violent reaction. We spent the hours after monitoring for bleeding. So far, so good, but given how Honey reacted last night, I'm going to say I think we might have found out what kills the mothers. If the babies are shifting on full moons, the trauma that must cause to the body..." Dr. Silver sounded fascinated. He felt sick.

"We have to abort it." It pained him to say it, but Honey's life was more important than an experiment.

"That is one option, which I presented to her."

He blinked. "What other option is there?"

"Keeping the child."

His mouth open and shut because he had no reply that didn't involve killing the doctor for the very suggestion.

Dr. Silver kept yapping. "Don't look so horrified. If the shifting of the child is the problem, then the simplest solution is to hide her away when there's a full moon."

"Will that be enough?"

"I don't know."

"And what we don't know might kill me." The soft addition came from Honey herself, standing at the door, wavering on her feet.

"You shouldn't be awake yet," Dr. Silver rebuked.

"I have to pee."

"I've got you, sweetheart." Ulric swept her into his arms and carried her. Dr. Silver wisely didn't object.

Honey tucked her head into his shoulder and whispered, "I'm sorry I called you crazy. In my defense...a werewolf. Wow."

"I wish I could have found a better way of telling you."

"Don't think it would have mattered," she admitted on a soft laugh. "Even now I'm having a hard time reconciling what I thought I knew versus what I saw."

"I'm still the same man."

She snorted. "Who runs around the woods, howling at the moon every few weeks."

"If it helps, I don't have fleas, and I'm housebroken."

"Oh, Ulric." She said nothing for a moment as he crossed the living area and up the stairs to the master. The dawn light brightened the windows.

He didn't set her down until they reached the bathroom. When he would have stood there to make sure she didn't fall, she cleared her throat.

"Um, some privacy please?"

He exited the bathroom to find Dr. Silver and Quinn waiting.

"What do you want now?" He couldn't help the grumpy tone.

The doctor held up a needle. "If she doesn't want to keep the child, then she doesn't have to."

"Are you insane?" he hissed.

"Are you ever happy? First you want to abort, and now you're acting pissy because I'm offering?"

The door to the bathroom opened, and Honey stared. "That's a big needle."

"Would you prefer a pill?"

"I'd prefer to not have something in my belly that wants to tear its way out. I saw how that went in the movies."

"I would do my best to ensure that didn't happen," Silver promised.

"How?"

"For one, the change is chemical based, which means it can be halted."

"With drugs?" asked Ulric.

"That's one option. But a simpler solution is keeping her out of moonlight. For extra security I'd even say avoid it a few days before and, as you progress, the day after."

"So become the opposite of a vampire and hide myself at night?"

"Only until the child is born."

"Nine months of house arrest? Great," was Honey's dull reply.

"It wouldn't have to be so stringent if you cooperated," Dr. Silver remarked.

"You locked me in this room."

"Because at the time you weren't listening."

"I am now," Honey huffed. "How many werewolf babies have you helped birth?"

"You'd be my first attempt."

Honey blinked. "You're kidding, right?"

"No. But keep in mind, the ban on Lycan pregnancy predates modern medical science."

Honey snorted. "How reassuring."

"You have a choice. We can remove the fetus right now." Dr. Silver waggled the needle. "Or we could monitor you with all the amenities we have access to."

Honey eyed the ultrasound unit Quinn held. "I want to see it before I decide."

"Worried you've got a puppy in there?" Silver teased as she pointed to bed.

"Yes." Honey didn't even pretend.

It worried him, too, hence why he positioned himself close to the bed. As she lifted her shirt for the wand and the squirt of gel, she reached for his hand. He clasped it and glanced at her. She bit her lip. He leaned down to whisper, "I'm here and will support whatever you want."

The screen came on, a jumble of dark shadows that moved around before fixating on the blob with the heartbeat.

It seemed bigger than when he'd seen it two days ago.

Honey bit her lip. "That's a real baby in there."

"Yes. No tail in sight," Silver quipped.

"Is it me, or am I further along than expected given it's been like two weeks? Am I going to have a shorter gestation?" Honey asked.

"It would appear that you will follow in the paws of canine pregnancy instead of human."

"For a wolf that's like two to three months, right?" she asked with a wrinkle of her brow.

Silver nodded.

Ulric had a question. "Won't growing a baby faster tax her body? It's my understanding a baby takes what it needs from its mother during pregnancy even at her detriment."

Once more Silver had a nod. "We should be able to prevent that with a high calorie diet and supplement with vitamins."

"A fast growth rate would explain my constant hunger," Honey murmured. She chewed her lip before asking, "These questions don't mean I've decided on a course of action."

"Of course. Tell you what, think it over and I'll be back later for your decision."

Silver left with Quinn, and Ulric cleared his throat. "Do you want me to go, too?"

She shook her head as she sat up. "Stay, please. I'm finding myself less angry now that I know you were at least telling the truth. I'm pregnant with a werewolf baby. Oh god." She flopped face down on the bed.

He crouched. "You don't have to be."

"I don't," she agreed, her reply muffled by the

comforter. She turned her head. "But the question is, can I terminate? There's a person inside me. A person we made. I don't know if I can abort."

"Even knowing it might kill you?"

"It's not the baby's fault. And Silver made a good point. Science has come a long way."

"Science hasn't dealt with werewolves."

"Then it might be a good time to start."

"Can't it start with someone else?" he grumbled, only to add, "I don't want to lose you."

"Are you sure? I was a right bitch to you."

"In your defense, my story was a tad hard to believe. Just a tad," he said, squishing his fingers together with a quirk of his lips.

"You really are a werewolf. Meaning you didn't lie to me." She sighed. "And you're not crazy. But I most certainly am." She closed her eyes as if exhausted.

"I'm sorry, Honey. I never expected any of this to happen."

"Then let me ask you, what did you imagine happening when you seduced me and told me you loved me? Were you going to disappear every full moon? Would you have ever told me you were neutered?"

"I don't have to shift on the full moon. I do it because it's fun. But if needed, I can stay inside and control it. As for the vasectomy, I had sperm frozen before I was changed."

"So you would have lied to me."

"I don't know. Some partners can handle the truth, some can't. Those that can't..." His lips turned down.

Her mouth rounded. "What happens to people who don't keep your secret?"

"Bad things."

Her jaw snapped shut.

"I would never harm you." He wouldn't, but he couldn't guarantee the others if she blabbed.

"Does it hurt?" she asked.

Not the question he'd expected. "Yes and no. It's painful euphoria. There is something almost orgasmic with setting the wolf free."

"And you're aware when the change happens?"

"Yes. But at the same time, I'm not the one in charge. The wolf is."

"Isn't the wolf you?"

"It's complicated." The best answer.

"Would you have ever told me if I hadn't gotten pregnant?"

"Honestly, I don't know. Some couples can survive the revelation. Not to mention revealing our secret is a pretty big deal."

"Which puts me in danger if I don't keep my mouth shut."

"Yes." He wouldn't lie. His love for her wouldn't save her if she exposed them.

"My parents will be worried sick about me."

"Your parents think I whisked you on an impromptu cruise with bad cell reception."

She stared at him until he admitted, "I know a guy who's good with hacking and deepfakes. He sent them some convincing images, messages, and even a staticky voicemail."

"A werewolf buddy?"

"Yeah."

"So there's more than just you obviously. How many?"

He shrugged. "I don't know. Our numbers vary from Pack to Pack."

She sighed. "This is a lot to absorb."

"I know."

She squeezed his hand. "Thanks for being patient with me."

"Thank you for listening and not running away screaming."

Her lips quirked. "Pretty sure you're faster than me."

"I'd rather you didn't bolt from me at all."

"Have I totally messed up things between us?"

"Never. I meant it when I told you there was a special connection between us."

"The baby."

He shook his head as he reached to stroke her cheek. "It existed before we even had sex. You're the one for me, Honeybee."

She reached out to trail her fingers across his jaw. "Can we rewind to the part where you made me ridiculously happy?"

"Yes."

"Even if I keep the baby?"

"I'm yours, no matter what."

"I want to talk to the doctor again."

Ulric thought of fetching Dr. Silver, but with Honey reaching out to mend the rift, he chose instead to say, "She's probably down in the kitchen. The dining room is her lab currently."

"Mmm. Kitchen means food. I could use a snack."

He grinned. "Bacon, eggs, and toast?"

"Pancakes, too, please?"

He outright laughed.

Maybe everything would be all right.

18

Honey didn't know if she'd be all right, but as she chewed on a hashbrown that Ulric scrounged from the freezer and deep fried to perfection, she had to admit at least she'd be well fed.

She sat at the large kitchen island with a plate laden with the promised eggs, bacon, and toast. A side plate held three fluffy pancakes drizzled with melted butter then syrup. Oh god, she just about drooled.

Thankfully, no one talked, meaning she could stuff her super hungry face. Like she'd never been this ravenous, not even those times she got high. She was so intent on eating everything in sight, she begrudged the tiny piece of bacon given to Terror.

Ulric sat across from her and kept her supplied with food. His buddy, Quinn—good-looking guy, wearing tactical gear that included a pistol in a holster tucked under his arm—ate standing up. Dr. Silver chewed absently while working on a laptop.

Only as she reached the end of her pile did Honey feel ready to converse. She did so less than subtly. "I'm keeping the baby."

Ulric never paused in his eating, but Quinn did. Dr. Silver didn't turn her head as she muttered, "I already figured that."

"Given that's the case, the more information I have the better. Starting with, are there any other triggers I should know about other than moonlight?" Honey asked, taking a sip of orange juice.

"Maybe." Dr. Silver half turned to eye her instead of her screen. "Keep in mind you're the first actual Lycan pregnancy I've been able to follow from almost conception. I'm going on hypothesis here."

"Not reassuring."

"Would you prefer I lie?" Dr. Silver offered.

She pursed her lips. "No, but a little bit of encouragement would be nice."

"I'm here, aren't I? I wouldn't bother if I thought I wasted my time."

"Your bedside manner sucks."

"I'm good at what I do. My personality shouldn't matter."

"Do you use that line on your dating profile?" Quinn quipped.

Dr. Silver shot him a glare. "Don't you have a job to do?"

"A job that involves watching over her." Quinn pointed at Honey.

"To make sure I don't run away?" she retorted.

"Actually, it's to protect you. Looks like the threat is all about you, Dr. Honey Iris." Quinn held out his phone. "I just got word the vet clinic was vandalized last night, as was your house."

Honey couldn't help the gasp. "Oh my god. No." At least they didn't have any overnight pets. But her practice...destroyed. Her home. Her things...

Ulric somehow managed to slide over the island to catch her before she fell off her stool. He swept her up and brought her to a couch but kept her in his lap, secure in his arms.

She could have protested, but she rather liked the spot. He held her up as she processed the news.

"Was anyone hurt?" she whispered.

Quinn shook his head. "No, but other than that, I have little info. Declan just sent me the notification. I'll give them a call and see if they have any extra info." The man left, and Dr. Silver rounded the couch to stand in front of her.

"If you're going to faint all the time, maybe you shouldn't go any further."

Honey glared at the doctor. "I'm allowed a moment to process."

"You've had it. Time to get to work."

"I thought you just wanted to examine me," grumbled Honey, not wanting to leave Ulric's lap quite yet.

She'd pretty much forgotten why she'd been so angry. He'd had good reason for his actions, although she remained unimpressed he'd accused her of cheating. Yes, from his point of view, she could see why, but from hers, he should have trusted her. Meaning they weren't good yet, but maybe they could be.

"I do want to examine you, but on a more thorough level given how closely we need to monitor you."

"And what if I do go into some kind of distress?" Honey asked.

"Depending on the kind, I'll act."

"That doesn't sound ominous at all," Honey opined with a roll of her eyes. "How about I avoid triggers, starting with moonlight. How much is too much? Is it only the full moon that affects the baby or a partial?"

"No clue." Dr. Silver couldn't give her a definite answer. "Could be only the full moon. Maybe it takes just a ray. Testing it would require you stand in it and see if it causes pain."

"We already know the full moon hurt." The sharp intensity of it left her with a cold chill. "When's the first sliver of it scheduled to appear so we can test?"

"Slow down. While I do agree we should find out, I also advise against it because triggering a shift might not be good for you or the baby."

"So the fetus is definitely a werewolf?" Ulric asked.

"Maybe."

"Would you stop it with the maybes?" Honey snapped.

"No." Dr. Silver didn't apologize. "We're in uncharted woods. Everything is a maybe."

Honey grimaced. "This is so crazy. I can't believe I went from having a normal life to wondering if I need a sleeper with a hole for a tail."

"The ultrasound showed no tail," Dr. Silver muttered.

"Again, you need to work on those pep talks."

Dr. Silver shrugged. "Not going to happen, nor can I make you guarantees about anything, only that I want to keep you and the child alive."

"Why?" Honey asked because she had to wonder why the woman cared. "I can't pay you."

"This isn't about money. It's about understanding the Lycan community."

"Why?" She sounded like a child on repeat.

"Because it is an exciting scientific discovery," Dr. Silver blatantly stated.

"That you can't tell anyone about."

"And? Not everything is about fame and glory. Some of us are genuinely curious."

"What the doc is admitting is she is a bona fide nerd," Quinn drawled, having silently returned.

"Says the meat puppet." Dr. Silver insulted Quinn without even looking around.

Honey cocked her head at Dr. Silver. "I have to admit that now that I'm not freaking out, I'm kind of curious too." She knew canines and other animals. Wolves weren't all that different in many respects.

"I could let you read some of the studies I've been conducting on the Lycans. It would be interesting to get your perspective."

Honey shoved upward from Ulric's grip. "I have to ask, are female Lycans sterilized as well so they don't get pregnant?"

It was Ulric who stated, "There are no females."

She stood and glanced back at him. "What do you mean none? Is it some sexist boy club where you only bite those with penises?"

"More like it doesn't work on women."

"You know this because it's been tried, or is it another werewolf legend?" she queried. How much about werewolves did she have wrong?

"It's been tried. Like tons. The bite does nothing."

She pursed her lips. "You'd better not be lying." Because she remembered much nibbling of flesh. She flushed and turned to the doctor. "When should we get started?"

"Whenever you're ready."

"Can someone ever be ready to be a science experiment?" Honey rolled her eyes, but not in rancor. She had a choice with this pregnancy. Abort and live with the guilt and the what-if the rest of her life or take a chance.

She chose life.

"Let me get some equipment set up in the bedroom. Give me like ten minutes. You." Dr. Silver pointed to Quinn. "Be useful and move some stuff for me."

She left with Quinn, and only Ulric remained. He stood, looming and solid.

She tilted her chin. "Talk after dinner? My room?"

"Anything you want, Honeybee."

"Good. See you later."

Because she wasn't just keeping this baby. She wanted the daddy too.

19

ULRIC SPENT that day in a state of anxiety. Honey had said they needed to talk.

Good talk? Bad talk? The let's-give-it-another-shot talk? He almost feared letting himself hope. The wait just about destroyed him. He wanted to drag her off somewhere private right now! But he didn't want to come off as desperate.

They ordered in dinner, but he couldn't have said what they ate or said. It was almost time to find out his fate.

When she excused herself after dessert, she cast him a quick glance. Why did his stomach clench?

When he did finally knock on her door, he'd convinced himself she wanted nothing do with him again. To his surprise, and relief, she dragged him inside and kissed him.

No words. Just sensual touch. Her hands tore at his

clothes, and he helped her, removing his shirt then hers. Their lips clung in between. Her breaths harsh and hot.

Out of control. He felt it. Wanted it as he crushed her to his bare frame. The heat of her sent a shiver zinging down his body.

She lay on the bed, his woman. His mate. Beckoning with her hands and pouty lips.

He covered her body with his, parting her thighs to nudge the core of her with the tip of his hard dick. She grabbed hold and drew a gasp from him as she intentionally used him to rub her clit. She moaned and rolled her hips under him as she gave herself pleasure. Using him to bring herself to a tiny orgasmic peak.

Even as she still hitched from that tiny climax, he slid into her slick sheath, feeling the tight walls of her channel clenching. Tightening. Pulling him deep and holding tight as he thrust and pulled.

Pushed. And tugged.

Pounded against her sweet spot as her nails dug into his back. She uttered soft, mewling cries as she bucked under him, her hips rolling in time to his thrusts. Begging him to slam deeper. Hard.

Fuck.

He came hard, his whole body bowed with the impact. His head went back in a silent scream. She held her breath as she went rigid.

He cradled her in his arms as she recovered, panting and whispering, "I missed you."

"Me too. I love you, Bee." The words he'd been aching to say since their separation.

"I love you, too." A declaration that eased his heart as she cupped his cheeks and tenderly kissed him.

They made love again, slowly. Sensuously. They woke intertwined, and he could have stayed snuggled like this forever.

Not Honey. She shoved and squeaked, "I've got to pee now."

She ran to the bathroom and emerged with a hungry eye. Not for his morning hard-on. Nope. His woman growled, "Bacon."

"Put some clothes on first!" he hollered as she aimed for the door.

"If I must." She dressed quickly, and he hurried to follow.

Once in the kitchen, he didn't even try to keep up with her appetite. She couldn't get enough. They split after the last donut disappeared, with her going to do science-y stuff with Silver, while he walked the perimeter with Quinn.

"So...you and the woman made up?" his friend remarked as they set out.

"Yeah."

"Remind me to never fall in love. It looks unpleasant." Quinn grimaced.

"Not when you meet the right woman."

"Which will never happen."

Ulric snorted. "It's like you want fate to bitch-slap you."

"She'd have to catch me first," Quinn joked.

"Did we ever get any more information on the break-ins at Honey's place and work?"

"Nope. No prints. No clues. But my guess is the office break-in is tied in to the guy you caught inside her place a few nights ago."

"You found out who he was?"

"Nope."

Ulric grimaced. "If only I hadn't accidentally killed him. We'd have answers."

"Maybe. Doesn't mean he would have talked."

"He would have talked," Ulric claimed ominously.

"In better news, we should be safe out here. Dorian's covered our tracks thoroughly."

If only Ulric could believe it.

20

Despite the oddity of the situation, and her rapidly expanding waistline, Honey had spent the last few weeks in almost heaven. She geeked out in the daytime, deep diving into Lycanthropy, the official term for those who turned into wolves.

Only men bitten by a Lycan could shift. Not all bites caused the change. Some people weren't affected at all. And a rarer few died.

To trigger the shift took a full moon unless you were what they classed an alpha. Alpha types could switch at will.

Given the danger caused by pregnancy, and before vasectomies became a thing, various things were done to prevent pregnancy from men taking concoctions to kill their sperm to their mates given potions for contraceptive, and if the worse happened? The women were forcibly aborted.

As science progressed, the rules adapted and insisted those bitten be sterilized either before the change or just after. Which explained Ulric's vasectomy. It was based on a rule enacted centuries ago by something called the Cabal, a shadowy group that oversaw the Packs around the world. Anonymous, chosen through unknown means, they were the ones who usually handled situations that might reveal the Lycan existence. The ones who gave permission for her to attempt to have this baby.

It chilled her to realize how close she might have come to losing the fetus, or even her life, via their machinations.

Because she knew their secret.

What the books and internet had to offer about werewolves differed in many respects from the observations noted by Erryn—Dr. Silver's first name—as they'd quickly progressed from doctor and patient to friends. A friendship that could get testy given their relative confinement and with her hormones going crazy. Why just yesterday Honey had burst into tears because Quinn returned from a supply run to town without her favorite donuts from Timmies.

Today? She itched in her own skin and wanted nothing to do with the daily poking, prodding, and measuring. For some reason, Erryn insisted on doing it every single day, which led to Honey asking, "Wouldn't it be more efficient to go weekly? There can't be much change in twenty-four hours."

"In a normal human pregnancy, no. But as you've observed, your pregnancy is far from normal. And need I remind you wolf gestation ranges from sixty days and up, and you're already at least 5 weeks, maybe a touch more. That puts you more than halfway."

Honey put a hand to her noticeable swell. The rest of her remained toned, even gaunt. The baby ate faster than she could. "I really hate it when you compare the baby to a puppy."

"Not my fault it's growing like one," Dr. Silver retorted.

A fact she tried to reconcile. In less than a month, she'd be a mom. If the baby lived.

If the fetus didn't kill her.

So many unknowns. She should have been terrified, only in her heart she knew she was doing the right thing. It helped that, thus far, other than the abnormal growth, everything else appeared fine. Her bloodwork came back a little low on some vitamins as the pregnancy took what it needed, but they were supplementing and monitoring to ensure nothing dropped precipitously.

She was eating all the time. Breakfast, lunch, dinner. Snack before lunch. Two in the afternoon. The evening she hugged a big bowl of popcorn and had growled when Ulric tried to grab a handful.

That man did his best to take care of her. And he did a great job. He also got the brunt of her severe hormonal mood swings.

"Don't breathe so loud." A common complaint when she awoke in the middle of the night, and he dared to inhale air. *"You don't want that potato, do you?"* And then once she'd eaten it, sobbing, *"You want me to get fat."*

Through it all, he remained patient. Loving. The sex was epic, and she wanted it almost as much as food.

They did it most often in bed, but a few times they'd gone out into the woods. On a blanket that kept off the chill from the coming fall, they made love and would lie intertwined, staring up at the sky as they talked.

She knew everything about him. His favorite color —lime green—his hockey team—the Toronto Maple Leafs—even the fact he'd always wanted a big family but it was just him and his older parents. Dead a long time now.

Honey was his opposite in many ways. She loved blue, couldn't stand hockey, and had a loving set of parents who doted on their only child.

It hurt when she called her mother and lied, but she couldn't tell them the truth of why she hadn't come for a visit in a while. She did the occasional video call but stuck mostly to texts because she hated not telling her mom everything.

The one good thing she did was layer in the idea her pregnancy was further along than expected. It meant rewinding her relationship to Ulric to an earlier time so that her mother wouldn't question how Ulric could be the father if the baby arrived too soon.

Which seemed likely.

An almost ten-month pregnancy usually squished down into possibly less than three. No wonder she craved a second breakfast. Why wasn't second breakfast a thing in the real world? The hobbits in *The Lord of Rings* got one.

So unfair.

"Are you hungry again?" Erryn asked, snapping Honey out of her mood.

"Is it that noticeable?" She wrinkled her nose even as her stomach gurgled, which led to the baby pushing at her abdomen and squirming. She'd started feeling it a week ago.

A baby with no name yet since they couldn't see it anymore. The sac surrounding it had turned into something the ultrasound couldn't penetrate. A stethoscope could still hear the baby's heartbeat, but there was no way of knowing what lurked inside.

She tried not to think of the fact that maybe she did carry a puppy.

With claws.

No. She couldn't think like that. She'd chosen to do this. She couldn't chicken out now. Couldn't kill the life inside her.

But she did have to be careful. "Pretty sure I can feel the full moon coming," she remarked. Early on, they'd discovered that while she felt uncomfortable in its partial rays, she didn't suffer any cramping. Thus far at least. But it was only days away now, and she tingled.

"You sure you still want to do the moon test this close to a full?" asked Erryn, slipping the measuring tape around her middle to compare her circumference to the previous day.

Another centimeter wider. Damn. Ulric had been rubbing lotion on her taut skin, but she saw the faint red and purple lines popping here and there.

"We need to know, the same way you keep measuring. I figure just a quick dip out the kitchen door. If I feel anything, I'll dive back inside and head for the basement." Which had been outfitted much more luxuriously in the last month, as Ulric worked on making it a more palatable space that included a real bed, as well as a sink and toilet, run off of the existing pipes. She wondered how they'd explain it to the rental agency, a dumb thing to worry about given her other issues.

"I'm sure if you even so much as look constipated Ulric will cart you off." Erryn rolled her eyes.

"He is a touch overprotective." Which she didn't mind at all. It was nice to be coddled.

Erryn put her on the treadmill next at a brisk pace to watch her blood pressure and heart rate. "How's things with your family?"

Honey had spoken to her about the interrogations she'd had to endure for taking an extended trip with a man they didn't know. And didn't she know that was how women disappeared?

The question led to Honey grimacing. "Given I've never gone this long without a visit, they're really starting to question my disappearance, even with the regular phone calls and pictures. My mom started in on me because I missed her kitchen sink spaghetti sauce." Made with all the leftover vegetables in the garden as they shut it down for the season. "I don't know how long I can keep putting them off." They'd created a story based on her practice being vandalized that led to Ulric whisking her away after their fake cruise for a vacation to cottage country while contractors fixed her clinic. And then they'd stayed longer because a local vet had taken ill and Honey offered to help out.

"Do you think they'll call the cops?"

"They might."

"How do we alleviate their fears?"

"Honestly, nothing short of seeing me in person."

"Leaving here comes with a lot of risk."

"Does it?" Honey asked. "Nothing's happened since the break-ins."

"Because they might be waiting for you to pop your head out."

"What makes you so sure?" Honey didn't know where Erryn's paranoia came from.

To her surprise, Erryn actually answered. "There are fractures within the Cabal."

"What are they split on?" How interesting and the first Erryn mentioned it.

"Some think it's time we updated some of our rules."

"But the other half likes things as they are." Honey made the jump of logic. "They're the ones who would stick to the 'no pregnancy' rule. But at the same time, why come after me if they think I won't survive anyhow?"

"Did that rogue want to kill you?" Erryn questioned. "Don't forget. Ulric interrupted before we ever discerned intent."

Honey pursed her lips. "I guess we don't know, but at the same time, it was one guy and nothing since. There must be a way to see my parents and reassure them I'm fine." Her phone calls were routed through a cell tower far from their location. She never gave her parents any actual details about where she was staying. Just made-up stories about cats she'd seen as the replacement vet.

Meanwhile, the only pet in the house—one very active feline—didn't require any kind of aid at all.

"If you go visit, what are the chances your mom keeps your face out of social media?" Mom liked to document every single life moment.

Ulric had been super apologetic, but as he pointed out, *"As a guy who specializes in security, there are a ton of problems with you going for a visit. The first and foremost being your mom posts everything. Your visit would be on there for anyone to see. What if it brings down danger on your family?"*

"I don't know if they'll stay patient much longer, not to mention how long do we need to hide?"

"Ask Ulric."

"I'm asking you because we both know you call the shots."

"The Cabal has tasked me with getting you through this pregnancy, and that includes keeping you safe from anyone who would attack."

"What if it was just a crime of chance with no bearing on me at all? Home invasions happen for all kinds of reasons."

"Are you really that desperate to see your family?"

Honey nodded. "I see my mom a few times a month usually. We usually get pedicures every third Saturday."

Erryn leaned back in her seat. "I think I have an idea for you to see your parents. What if we brought them here?"

The suggestion rounded Honey's mouth. "Here?"

"Yes. Just the two of them, brought via a roundabout route."

The idea excited, but Honey quickly sobered. "Won't they think it's weird when they realize we never leave and that you and Quinn are living with us?"

"I'll be Ulric's sister. Quinn can pretend to be my boyfriend for a few days," Erryn suggested.

"Aren't you worried they'll be followed?"

"We can handle that part by ensuring we get them an escort and having Dorian play with their vehicle's nav system. We'll also get their phone signals redirected before they leave."

"How soon can I see them?" She couldn't deny being eager.

"We'll have to coordinate with Quinn. I'd say just after the full moon."

Only things didn't work out as planned.

21

THE PHONE CALL came the day before the full moon. Honey's mom was hysterical. Ulric only caught bits and pieces as Honey paced and asked low questions as she squeezed her eyes shut.

"...what hospital is he in?" Pause. Honey's mouth rounded as she exclaimed, "What do you mean he's at home? What exactly is wrong with him?"

"You have to come right away," was all her mother said before she hung up.

"What the fuck?" A rare expletive left Honey's lips. She dialed her mother right back. No one answered.

She shot him a glance. "Something is wrong."

"Yes." No denying it, even as the whole thing smelled off to him.

"Mom said Dad hurt himself. And that it was

urgent. I had to come right away. But if he's injured, why is he at home?" She flung her hands.

He pointed out the obvious. "Because it's a story to lure us."

She whirled to eye him. "Duh. I know that. None of what she said made sense, which is why we have to go."

"We?" He huffed. "You aren't going anywhere."

"You don't get to tell me what I can or cannot do. It's my parents." She dialed again. It answered to a whining screech that had her holding the cellphone away from her head. It then went silent.

She brought it back into view and muttered, "My phone just died." As in wouldn't even turn on. She tried plugging it in to charge, but even that did nothing to revive it.

Ulric knew then and there he had no choice. Even as the protector in him screamed, *trap!* he dragged her close and murmured, "Pack an overnight bag. We're going on a road trip."

The news didn't go over well with the doctor.

"Excuse me, but you can't do that," Silver retorted.

"Weren't you the one who told her you'd make something happen?"

"After the full moon," Erryn advised. "Which is tomorrow night. That doesn't give you much time to drive there and get back."

"You're positive the baby is going to react to the moon?" he asked.

Erryn nodded.

"Then I make sure she stays inside, and we don't expose her to the moon at all. The same plan we had for here."

"You know it's a trap."

"Or an opportunity. Honey can't hide in the woods forever. If this is a ploy to ambush, then we'll be ready for it."

"You're taking a risk with her and the baby."

"I know, but I also know it would destroy her mentally if something happened to her parents and she didn't even try." Ulric couldn't do that to her. He would hate it if someone did it to him.

"It's too dangerous," Erryn snapped. "I'll go talk to her."

"There is nothing to say." Honey appeared, carrying a knapsack. "You don't get to tell me what to do. I am a grown-ass woman, and my parents need me. So you can fuck off if you think I'm going to stay away. And for your information, I am not a child or an idiot. I am aware the full moon is coming. My parents have a rec-room in the basement with the only window covered over and soundproofed because my dad likes to watch movies in comfort at home. Now, if you're done harassing my boyfriend, I need to grab some food for the road. If we leave now, we'll be there by late afternoon." She eyed him. "I grabbed a few of your things too. Quinn and Erryn will take care of Terror while we're gone because my mom will murder us if we bring home a cat." With those orders thrown, she stalked out of the house.

Ulric blinked.

Quinn whistled. "Damn. Fun car ride."

Actually, Ulric wasn't worried. He'd been advocating for Honey. Not that Honey needed his help. She was one hell of a woman.

"I'm hungry!" she bellowed from outside. "We need to hit a drive-through."

Ulric shrugged. "Gotta go. You heard her. Baby is hungry."

"You know we're going to follow you," Erryn hissed.

"In that case, don't forget Terror hates being in the carrier, but if you bring his litter box, he should be okay. He has nervous shits," Ulric relayed as he followed Honey out the door. He headed for the SUV, noting she'd chosen the passenger seat.

She had her hand in a bag of chips he'd left stashed in the truck for an emergency since their last grocery run.

He slid into the driver's seat and buckled up.

"Thanks for not arguing," she stated.

"I'll always be on your side, Bee."

He wasn't about to stand in her way but rather by her side. Because what if there truly was something wrong with her father? Something grievous. She'd never forgive him if she couldn't be by her dad's side.

Hell, he'd never forgive himself.

It made for a stressful trip, with Honey cursing her dead phone. He wouldn't let her try calling with his because as he reminded, "We're in the boonies. It's our online lifeline if something happens. We can't risk frying it too."

"Don't be crazy. It was a fluke."

Was it? He could have sworn he'd heard Dorian mention how to wipe a phone remotely by sending it some weird code via a phone call that caused it to overload. "We can't take the chance." Bad enough they'd left their safe house. The fact her phone might have been intentionally targeted? Even scarier. They could be driving into a trap. But he had no choice.

She pouted. He didn't relent. On this, he would take precautions. Part of not being noticed involved driving just over the speed limit so they didn't stand out. Honey didn't like that either. "You drive slower than my grandma."

They paid for everything in cash—one tank of gas with snacks, plus two stops for fast food and bathrooms. He didn't doubt Quinn followed with Erryn and probably caught up due to their frequent stops. While he'd not seen signs of a tail, that didn't mean they weren't there.

Honey sat in the passenger seat, taut with anxiety. Drumming her fingers. Pursing and blowing her lips.

She was the one who'd muttered, "If Dad was hurt, why would he be at home? Unless someone injured him and won't let him leave."

He knew what she thought. What they all thought. Another attack by whoever sent the first thug and then vandalized her home and office.

The questions being, why and who gave the orders?

Rather than dwell on it, he tried to lighten the mood. "So, do you think your parents will like me?"

She snorted. "Nope. You'd better hope my dad is too sick to shoot."

"Wait, what?"

"Did I not mention he's a gun fanatic? He's got a huge collection."

"I thought he was an accountant."

"He is. One who likes to shoot things. Expect venison roast in the fall."

"Doesn't sound like your dad is the type to be ambushed easily."

"I don't know. I mean it's a whole different thing to be in the woods waiting in a blind to shoot a deer or turkey than it is to have someone come into your suburban home. My mom would probably guilt them."

He chuckled.

"Don't laugh. You wait until she starts in on you."

"Why would she come after me?"

Honey glanced at her belly. "Do I really need to explain?"

"Oh. Is it a big deal you're pregnant?"

"It's a big deal I'm not married but am pregnant.

My mother's moaning how she'll be the only one of her sisters to have a bastard grandchild."

"Who cares nowadays?"

"My mother."

He thought of the box he had tucked in the glove box. "It will be fine." What he said, but inside he kept practicing what he'd say when he showed it to Honey.

He pulled into the large driveaway, empty of vehicles.

Honey frowned at the home.

"What's wrong?" he asked.

"Looks a little too normal."

He agreed. "Can you give me a second to scout before you go inside?"

She nodded.

A relief because the calm raised the hairs on his neck. "Stay in the car until I tell you it's safe."

He approached the front of the house with its nicely tended shrubs, some of them covered in burlap tents for the impending winter. He heard a television playing from the window partially concealed by the oversized lilac bush with its gnarly branches stubbornly clinging to a few brown leaves.

"Both their cars are in the garage," she announced.

He whirled to see her on tiptoe, peeking in the windows.

"What are you doing? I told you to stay in the car," he hissed loudly as he waved his hands.

"I was bored. Besides, I can smell Mom's cooking." She tilted her head back and inhaled.

What was she talking... Oh. The aroma hit him. Tantalizing and giving him a sudden hunger. How had she smelled it first, though?

"We can go inside," she announced.

"You said I could look around."

"You did and good job, but if Mom's cooking, everything is fine. She won't cook under duress." Honey joined him as she said it then moved past him to the door. She didn't ring the bell or even knock, just grabbed the handle to walk in, hollering, "I'm here!"

Ulric moved quickly to keep up, wanting to dive ahead of her to act as a shield; however, short of shoving his pregnant mate, he could do nothing but follow.

The television blared, and a glance in the living room showed it empty.

"Mom! Mommyyyy!" Honey hollered impressively. Then winked at him. "I should have warned you; we're the loud family."

"Just how many more secrets do you have, Honeybee?"

"Tons." She grinned so mischievously she almost popped a dimple. "Jealous that you're not the only one?"

"More like delighted there's so much of you left to discover." He smiled down on her and would have planted a kiss, only he heard someone reply.

"Stop bellowing. I'm coming!" bellowed a woman who emerged through a swinging door at the far end of the wide hall. A shorter, rounder, older version of Honey, she wiped her hands on an apron dusty with flour.

"Where's Daddy?" Honey asked upon seeing her.

"Excuse me? Where's, 'Hello, Mommy? How are you? Sorry I've been a neglectful daughter,'" the woman berated.

"Neglectful how? We talk almost every single day," Honey huffed.

"Talk yes, but do you visit? No. It's like you don't love me anymore. Me, who sacrificed my girlish figure. Untold sleepless nights. And that head. Aie. No love." Honey's mother managed a melodramatic fling.

Honey didn't fall for it. "Where's Daddy?"

"Around, but I don't know if he wants to see you."

Honey's gaze narrowed. "Hold on, are you telling me there's nothing wrong with him?"

"Other than the usual?" riposted her mother.

"You faked that phone call! Why? Why would you panic me like that?" Honey freaked.

"You know why." Mom's gaze went to Ulric then Honey's belly. Then narrowed on him again. "Well. Well. Look who finally found the balls to be a man and show his face."

"Mom!" Honey exclaimed. Meanwhile, Ulric really wished he'd stayed in the car.

"He's not welcome here." Honey's mom crossed her arms and glared.

"Don't be ridiculous." Honey tucked close and grabbed his hand. "The reason you didn't meet him before was because I didn't want to share him quite yet. So don't blame Ulric. It's not his fault. Things just kind of happened."

"Apparently," her mom replied dryly, along with another stare at Honey's rounded belly.

"Don't start, Mom. I'm a grown woman. My body, my choice, remember?"

"Is it? It's been so long since I've seen you." Mom went back to the other guilt trip.

"We're here now, even if on false pretenses. Happy? Mom, this is Ulric. Ulric, this is my mom, Daisy Iris."

He had practice not chuckling at the name because one of his good friends was called Billy Gruff. "Nice to meet you, Mrs. Iris."

"Nice? Ha!" she snorted. "Steals my daughter away for more than a month. Brings her back looking like she's starving. Which means my grandbaby is probably dying of hunger, and you think you can charm me?"

"I swear, I feed her often, but I'm a pretty basic cook."

"You make food for her?" The mother eyed him. "Like what?"

"Steak. Burgers. Chops. I'm handiest around a barbecue."

"I like barbecue," stated Mrs. Iris.

"Honey and I would love to serve you some when you come to dinner." He smiled.

He didn't get one in return, just a terse, "We eat in ten minutes." The woman whirled and stomped into the kitchen.

Honey eyed him. "She must like you."

"How do you figure? She just reamed me out."

"She offered you dinner."

"Which makes me happier than you'll ever know." Since they'd walked inside, his nose wanted to follow the aroma. His taste buds watered.

"I can't believe she tricked us into coming," Honey grumbled as she kicked off her shoes.

"I will admit, I didn't have completely fake emergency on my bingo card." And yet as he kicked off his shoes, he'd never been more relieved. At the same time, how did her parents have access to the kind of tech that could wipe a phone? The same kind with the balls to fake an emergency.

A glance to the room opposite that of the television showed a second living room, much more ornate in décor, with the carved sofa and end tables, porcelain bric-a-brac all over, and every single piece of fabric-covered furniture glossy with plastic.

He inclined his head and asked, "Is that to protect the furniture from pets?"

Honey snorted. "As if my mom would ever allow an animal inside. She usually runs a lint roller over me the moment I walk in the house. Why do you think I told you to leave the cat with Erryn and Quinn?"

"Wait a second." He snapped his fingers. "Was becoming a vet a rebellion thing for you?"

One corner of her mouth quirked. "Maybe."

"Nerd," he teased.

"Be glad of it or we would have never met," she taunted right back.

He dragged her close, entranced by the way she'd found her smile again. "We would have met. Fate would have intervened."

As they passed the door in a hall smelling faintly of exhaust, which must lead to the garage, he had to wonder, "Where's your father?"

"Probably up to no good," Honey muttered. "Be ready."

The door behind them opened.

Ulric smelt the gun oil before the man holding it. He whirled and made sure he acted as a shield for Honey as he slapped away the hand holding the barrel of a shotgun. "Honey, get out of here."

"Don't hit him!" Honey shrieked as he wound back his fist to punch. She also added, "Daddy, put that gun down!"

Daddy? He eyed the older fellow in front of him. Almost of a size as Ulric, thicker around the middle, his hair white with a few hints of gray. Scowling at Ulric with Honey's eyes.

Dammit.

Ulric stepped away from Honey's dad, who once more placed both hands on the gun and aimed it.

Honey didn't pay it any kind of respect. "What do you think you're doing?" She stepped in front of the barrel, and the man immediately dropped it down.

"It wasn't loaded."

"And yet what was the rule you taught me growing up? Hunh?" Honey wagged a finger in his face and harangued, "You said, 'Don't let me catch you aimin' it at anyone, or you're in trouble.'"

"He deserved a little scare." The glare was for Ulric.

"Ulric hasn't done anything."

"I wouldn't call what he did nothing. And then he steals you away. Haven't seen you in months—"

"It's been one, Daddy."

"Seems longer," he grumbled eyeing her large belly. "And then you show up with the control freak. I wanted to make sure he wasn't holding you hostage." The glare would have incinerated Ulric if the man had superpowers.

"I am his girlfriend, not his prisoner," Honey huffed.

"I swear, sir, my intentions are honorable." He tried to defend himself.

"And yet my unmarried daughter is getting close to popping your brat." The other man arched a brow.

Honey huffed. "Seriously, Daddy. I told you it wasn't his fault. My IUD fell out."

"Argh. My ears. Daisy," the man bellowed his way into the kitchen.

Honey sighed. "I'm sorry."

"For what? The fact your parents are overprotective?"

"No, not sorry for that. It kind of comes with the whole being-with-me package. I am apologizing for what they're about to do next."

She didn't elaborate. He experienced it at the dinner table as he got grilled on his life, his prospects—

"So a security guard for a marijuana shop. Not exactly lofty goals."

"An apartment is much too small for a growing family."

—bank account—

"You'd think a man your age would have put more away."

—and his intentions.

"Have you been married? What do you think of marriage? Kids? The church?"

He gladly replied over the most delicious roast he'd ever had in his life

When Mrs. Iris point-blank said, "I can't believe my daughter is going to have a bastard," Ulric slipped from his chair and pulled a box from his pocket, the one he'd kept stashed in the dash since Quinn went for a visit to Ottawa. Ulric got him to bring his mother's old wedding bands, passed down in the family and glittering after soaking in Coke for a day.

He hit a knee and kept it simple. "I love you. Marry me."

22

Honey pretended to think about it.

Daddy thought it was funny to whisper, "He's only doing it 'cause he knows I'll bring out the shotgun."

Which led to Mommy tossing a Yorkshire pudding at her husband, who caught it and exclaimed, "Don't be throwing good food away. I was planning on having this for lunch tomorrow."

Leaning her forehead against Ulric's, Honey murmured, "You sure you still want to marry me after having seen my family is majorly crazy?"

"I will always want to be with you."

Her yes was a kiss, which led to gagging from Daddy and drama as he clutched his chest, gasping, "My heart."

Mommy slapped him on her way to hug Honey and exclaimed, "I'll call Yvette for a dress appointment in the morning."

"We have to leave in the morning," Honey announced. "I have to be somewhere by midafternoon."

"Leave?" Mommy's shoulders flattened. "But you just got here."

"Because you faked an injury. However, it doesn't change the fact I was in the middle of something." Honey stood her ground because she knew to waver would lead to her parents dominating.

Mommy tried. "More important than family?"

"I've got my own family to take care of now." She put a hand on her stomach, which led to her mother harrumphing.

Her father chimed in. "I will call the church and get the first available Saturday."

"The first?" Honey squeaked. "Isn't that fast?"

"If you wanted leisurely, you should have kept your legs shut. If you can't stay, I'll take measurements and have Yvette put something together with flounces we can adjust in case you actually start eating right."

Flounces? "I can shop for my own dress."

"You do that while I find a venue to accommodate on short notice. It will need to seat at least two hundred. But that would really be trimming the list."

"Can't we do something simple?" Honey lamented.

Mommy and Daddy both laughed.

Ulric leaned close to whisper, "Okay, now I'm freaked out."

"This is just the start," was her ominous reply.

They didn't really get a chance to speak alone until Daddy went out for a cigarette and Mommy went looking for her wedding binder, which she'd been keeping since Honey was a kid.

"Exactly how fancy are we looking at for this wedding?" he asked when she collapsed against him.

"Tux. White dress. Church—"

"Church? But we're not religious."

"Neither are they, but they do like to follow certain traditions. Should have seen my dad lose it when the church we used regularly refused to marry his older sister, Kay, and her partner, Leanne. By the time my dad was done freaking out, Pastor Frank decided it was best he transferred to another parish."

"Is this your way of telling me he wasn't joking about a shotgun wedding?"

"You could always refuse and he'll get the shovel," she added with a grin.

"As if I wanted to escape. You're stuck with me, Bee." He nuzzled her neck, and she sighed against him.

"Thanks for bringing me. I know you didn't really want to."

"You'd have never forgiven me if something happened to your parents."

"My parents, who should have been terrible actors." She glared at the walls as if she could see and laser them through it.

"Is this a taste of them as grandparents?"

"Actually, they will be great grandparents. I can see

them stealing the child often, giving us alone time. Spoiling it rotten. But when it comes to being in-laws..." She shook her head. "Sorry to say you're screwed."

"Don't be so sure. I thought we were getting along pretty good there at the end."

"That's just how they suck you in. Be on guard. Oh, and don't make a big deal of the fact you have to sleep on the couch. My mom told me that until we were married, it was her job to chaperone us."

"Kind of late, isn't it?"

"That's what I said. But she wouldn't budge."

"At least you argued. Your dad told me if he caught me in your room, they would not find enough of me to identify." At the time, they'd been puffing on an after-dinner cigar that really tasted good after that epic feast. Who knew a nicely rolled stogy went well with the glass of port?

"He said what?"

"It's no big deal, Bee. Just guy talk."

"That's all you have to say? Aren't you a little freaked out? I mean you were told to marry me, or my dad will hunt you down and shoot you."

A grin tugged his lips. "Is it weird I like that about him? I mean, if I had a daughter, I'd probably do the same thing."

"Do you want a girl?"

"Only if she's just like you."

"A nerd?" she teased.

"Is that what they call perfection?"

"I'm going to miss snuggling," she murmured, her head leaning against him.

"At least it's just for one night."

"Maybe two."

"What?"

She bit her lip. "Mom really wants to go dress shopping tomorrow. She's determined to have us wed before the baby pops."

He wanted to remind her the full moon was tomorrow night, but in this moment, he wanted to keep her happy and excited. Shopping for a wedding dress would only make what he knew official. "Go shopping. But stick to public places."

She stared at him before throwing herself in his arms for a kiss. "I love you," she murmured against his mouth.

"You are my everything, Bee," was his reply. And that was as far as things went as a throat cleared.

Daddy glowered. "Bedtime."

"Yes, Daddy."

"I'm getting my evening tea." Which was code for *Get upstairs before I come back*.

The moment Daddy disappeared, she was back in Ulric's arms, giving him a kiss. And another. She heard a distant thud.

Time was up.

She cast Ulric an apologetic glance. He grinned and mouthed, *Unlock your window*.

Her mouth rounded as she skipped up the stairs. Would Ulric really take that chance?

Probably.

And she loved him for it because she didn't want to sleep alone. She'd gotten used to using him as a body pillow made of rock.

Teeth brushed, first pee of the night accomplished, she climbed into her childhood bed. Her room had remained the same once she moved out. Mommy's way of showing she always had a place to come home.

Her gable room was tucked over the front door with its porch. The window unlatched and opened easily. The screen was something Ulric popped when he appeared a half-hour later.

She whispered, "You're so bad. What if my dad checks on you?"

"I lumped the blankets to look like a body."

"You're a pro at sneaking around, are you?"

"Only with you, Bee."

They made love in her bed, the narrow mattress requiring her to be on top, which she didn't mind. The carpet at least kept the bed from squeaking on the floor. His mouth caught her sounds of pleasure as she rocked and rolled atop him, her hips undulating to drive him deeper. The pressure just right. When her orgasm hit, she flopped on him and bit his shoulder rather than yell.

By the time he left her bed, she drowsed, only to wake suddenly starved and parched.

She snuck downstairs and peeked into the living room and noted the big lump on the couch. Ulric slept. She'd have to chew softly so as to not wake him.

In the kitchen, she struggled with what she wanted to eat. Her gaze strayed to the window overlooking Mom's garden. It probably still had some rhubarb. Mmm. Rhubarb smeared in peanut butter dipped in sugar.

Before heading outside, she glanced to the living room where Ulric slept. He'd be mad if she went out without waking him. At the same time, she just wanted a snack. In and out.

She disarmed the house alarm, wincing at each beep, and yet a glance at the couch showed his lumpy shape unmoving. She headed out the front and then to the side of the house where the big rhubarb plant had been widening since she was a child. She crouched to peruse the rhubarb stalks and had reached for one when she heard it. The rustle of fabric as if someone snuck up behind.

By the time she thought it, a gloved hand had been shoved over her mouth.

23

Ulric knew better than to get caught in Honey's bed. Her father—who didn't appear keen to have Ulric address him as anything other than sir—would most likely shoot him and bury him somewhere in his backyard if he thought for one moment Ulric disrespected his daughter.

The lure of his mate proved stronger than his fear of death, hence why he lingered close to her until the wee hours of two. She slept, her breathing soft and even, relaxed, and so beautiful it almost hurt.

He wanted nothing more than to stay close. To wake by her side. To see that little smile she always had when she first opened her eyes and saw him.

It was just for one night.

He'd live.

Right?

Departing by the window meant he could only

pull down the pane, not lock it. Surely she'd be fine. No one knew they were here, and in a few hours, dawn would arrive, and the street would be too busy for anyone to think of using it to climb in.

The bathroom window also remained unlocked, a fact that led to him doing a quick circuit of the main floor, padding barefoot and silent. He didn't see any signs anyone had entered. Smelled nothing untoward, only lingering tobacco smoke.

Had her father come down to check on him? The lump he'd left on the couch appeared undisturbed.

Until he pulled back the blanket.

The scowl that met Ulric just about ruined his masculinity. A good thing he'd peed not long ago.

"Uh." Ulric's brilliant defense at finding Honey's father on the couch.

"You've got a lot of nerve," the other man said, sitting up.

Ulric had no defense. A father had every right to be pissed. Ulric would deserve whatever punishment he meted. Knowing all this, he still had to apologize for disrespecting Honey's father. "Sorry isn't enough sir. I'll go sleep in my car."

"I'm not talking about that. I expected you to sneak off. It was my wife's idea. Said it was romantic." Mr. Iris snorted. "I am more pissed that you think you can just ask my daughter to marry her without speaking to me first."

"I was planning to. It's why I'd brought the ring in

the first place." He'd figured if he was going to meet his father's mate, he should do things right. "But at the time, the situation seemed to call for a grand gesture."

The other man nodded. "Yeah, Honey's mom kind of trapped you there."

"Let's pretend we had this conversation earlier. Sir"—Ulric stood straight and serious—"I really love your daughter. I would do anything for her. With your permission, I'd like her to be my wife."

Honey's dad snorted. "As if she cares what I think. My Honey has always been headstrong."

"I noticed."

The older man snorted. "Marry her. But hurt her and know that I will shoot you."

"Noted and not a concern, as I plan to spoil Honey." Once she survived the pregnancy. It was hard not to be nervous. Silver might be confident, but at the same time, it had been too easy thus far. The next full moon, only a day away, could be the trigger. He could feel his pulse pounding to a wilder beat. The tension coiling within.

The change was coming. Would Honey feel it too?

A pair of headlights momentarily lit the filmy curtains that hung over the bay window.

"Late for anyone to be out," Mr. Iris noted, moving closer to the window to look.

Ulric didn't think he was being too paranoid. "Did they keep going?"

"Yeah."

No one parked, and yet unease settled.

"I need a smoke." Honey's dad headed for the rear sliding door to the yard.

"Mind if I join you, sir?"

"Might as well call me Jacob seeing as how we'll be family soon."

The large yard held a stone patio, empty as the furniture had been covered and stowed for winter.

Jacob lit up, and Ulric joined him. He wasn't about to become a regular smoker, but there was something calming about the habit as they stood there, first in silence.

Jacob broke it first. "Working where you do, you'll have seen some of the seamier sides of business, correct?"

A creased marred Ulric's brow. "Lanark Leaf might sell pot products, but it is one hundred percent legal."

"Yes, of course." Jacob waved his cigarette before taking a draw. "But even legal companies sometimes deal with shady people."

"I'm assuming there's a point to this." Ulric remained cautious.

"I'm going to be blunt. I've made an enemy with my work."

"As an accountant?" Which quite honestly didn't match the bullish man in front of him. A man who wore a sweater that didn't completely hide the bulge of a revolver strapped to him.

"Don't sound surprised. An accountant knows more secrets than anyone else. It makes us dangerous. Especially when we work for people who skate dangerously on the edge of laws." The obliqueness didn't hide what Jacob meant.

"Wait, are you saying you do business with criminals?" Ulric exclaimed.

"Don't act so shocked. Especially since you've been tied into a few shady things of your own. Bar fights, really?"

His stomach sank. "You did a background on me."

"You knocked up my daughter. You're lucky that's all I did." Jacob took another drag.

"I will make her a good husband."

"Will you keep her safe?"

"That goes without saying," Ulric hotly stated.

"Good. Leave in the morning. I don't think they'll follow you, but don't take a direct route and make sure you're not tailed. It's probably being over cautious, but at the same time, I ain't taking the chance he'll use her to get to me."

"Excuse me?" The conversation had veered.

Mr. Iris stared at him with a serious mien. "You need to leave and watch over Honey until I settle a problem with Viper."

"Who the fuck is Viper?"

"Someone who wants me gone because I know too much."

"You knew this and yet let us stay the night?" Ulric growled.

"I didn't have much of a choice given what Daisy did to get Honey to come. I was actually glad my girl went off-grid. Was hoping I'd have my troubles sorted before she came back."

"Are you in trouble, sir?"

"Yes and no. Only Viper might want me dead, but the others that I work for don't, which means I've got some protection."

"If you were worried about your safety, you wouldn't be out here having a smoke. A sniper could take you out."

"We're in upper-class suburbia. There are cameras everywhere. Motion detectors too." Jacob waved a hand. "Anyone coming through the back would get lit up like the Fourth of July. You should see the chaos when the Fergusons forget to disarm theirs and let their dog out."

"They could be watching, waiting for an opportune moment."

"Neighborhood Watch calls bylaw on any vehicle's that parked more than three hours in the daytime, and they are not afraid to take note of the license plates of those staying overnight."

"Better than a gated community," Ulric muttered. Yet his unease remained. Something didn't feel right. "I should try and get a few hours' sleep." He was headed for the sliding door when he heard it.

A cry. He glanced at Jacob, who dropped his cigarette as he started sprinting for the front of the house.

Ulric was at his heels. The gate swung open, and Ulric heard another cry.

Honey!

They emerged into the front yard in time to see a struggling person being shoved into a car parked across the way on the corner with the giant hedges. The door slammed shut before Ulric had gotten halfway across the road.

The car sped off, the electric motor so quiet he'd not heard it in the yard.

"We have to follow." He bolted for the front door and spent a few precious minutes trying to locate his keys, which turned out to be on the floor under the couch, must have fallen from his pocket. By the time, he found them and sat in his car, with her father in the passenger seat telling him to move, he had no idea where to go.

Someone took his Honey.

Hopefully none of the neighbors heard the howling.

24

Honey stopped struggling with her first assailant when the barrel of a gun pressed to her forehead. "Get in the car."

A second kidnapper joined the first. The tough guys attacking a pregnant woman wore balaclavas to hide their features. She knew better than to go anywhere with them. That would lead to certain death.

"What do you want?" she asked as she gauged her ability to race back to the house. If she could just wake her daddy... He'd come to her rescue, guns blazing.

"Move," the guy with the gun snapped.

Her lips pursed. "I am not leaving with you." She knew better than to listen.

"I will shoot you."

"Fire it and see what happens," she taunted a little louder. Her father would hear a gunshot.

Would he hear her yelp when she didn't move quick enough to defend against the sudden violent blow? The pistol cracked the side of her head. Her eyes struggled to remain open as her knees buckled.

Before she could even blink, she was literally tossed into the car.

The sudden violent movement stole her voice. She would have scrambled out the other side if a beast of a man who didn't smell very nice joined her in the back. He lunged and grabbed a fistful of hair. "Make a sound and I'll scalp you."

It might still happen, given he didn't relent on the pressure. She felt strands snapping at the tension. *Ping.* Ouch. *Ping.* Ouch.

Gun Boy had the wheel, and he took off like a silent bat out of hell. Literally so quiet it had to be an electric car.

She wanted to ask questions. Beg for mercy. Pretend a bravery she didn't feel at the moment.

Her hands palmed her rounded belly, wondering if the men even cared she was pregnant. Obviously not. They'd had no problems threatening and manhandling her.

That callousness more than anything led to her blurting out, "Who are you? Where are you taking me?"

"Quiet."

"I'll be quiet if you tell me. I just want to know what's going on."

Rather than reply, the car halted, but only long enough for them to tie Honey's hands behind her back, gag her, and stuff her in the trunk.

A pregnant woman.

How low could these people go?

The ride lasted long enough her bladder hurt. All of her ached. She shivered as if feverish.

When the car finally stopped and the trunk was popped, she almost cried. Not that she was offered any relief.

Rough hands dragged her out and brought her into a house. She got a brief glimpse of hardwood floors and timber construction before being dragged down into a cement-block cellar.

They removed her wrist ties and the gag and instead tethered her, via chain collar, to a metal support post and left. No food. No water. Not even a pot to piss in. She had to squat as far as the chain would allow and let loose.

She'd been kidnapped, and given the treatment thus far, whatever they had planned for her wouldn't be pleasant.

The concrete floor provided no warmth or comfort, so she paced. And paced. It only led to increasing her fatigue. She slumped to the floor at one point and waited. Waited. Was it hours or days? She couldn't tell with the lack of windows. She did know that she hungered. Her stomach cramped, and thirst desiccated her mouth.

She'd long ago given up trying to break the chain that kept her. The loops proved impervious to tugging, the lock cinching it around her neck impossible to pick.

No one came no matter how much she screamed, "Let me out."

She hit the point of delirium, so dehydrated her eyelids felt like sandpaper. She wouldn't last long without sustenance. The baby needed to eat. She eyed her arm. If she ate herself, would it save the child...?

That was crazy talk.

The thud of steps on the stairs lifted her head. She beheld a stranger, slim of build, with a mustache darker than his silver-streaked hair, holding a bottle of water.

She wanted it. "Who are you?" she asked, instead of begging for the water.

"You are Honey Iris." Stated, not asked.

Lying would serve no purpose. "That's me. Why have you kidnapped me?"

"Because I need you to teach someone a lesson about breaking the rules."

"Who?"

"Don't play stupid. You know who, and it's time he paid."

"Listen, I don't know what your problem is, but I'm not involved. And I'm pregnant," she blurted out.

"Which is a shame," he said with a shake of his head. "It will slow you down."

"Slow me down for what?" She tried not to give in to the fear that wanted her to scream.

"The chase that is coming. See, you know too much. Have seen too much. Which means that even though he agreed to the trade, you can't live."

Her heart stopped. "You're going to kill me?"

"Oh yes. And let me reassure you that even if you weren't slow and fat from the pregnancy, you still wouldn't have been able to escape me." The man smiled, his teeth a little sharper than when he'd entered, his features somehow more angular and his jaw protruding.

She took a step back. "What are you?" Asked even as she had a feeling she knew.

"As if your shivering human body doesn't know."

"You're a monster," she huffed.

"I am top of the food pyramid. A predator with no match." He took a step closer. "Which is why your father shouldn't have—"

She interrupted. "My father? This is about him?"

"Don't play stupid. Who else would this be about but my so-called accountant who ratted me out?" the man grumbled. "As if I could let that stand. He's about to learn why he shouldn't have fucked with me. He must love you. He's on his way right now to exchange himself for you."

"I won't let you hurt my daddy." A brave, if useless promise to make.

"Whatcha going to do? Scream? Please do. Nothing better than a bit of music to accompany the hunt and the kill." The smile sickened her.

"Kill?" She repeated the word through numb lips. "I'm pregnant." She threw it out there in the hopes it made a difference.

"Then I guess you better run fast. Only way you live 'til morning is if you keep out of my grasp." He unlocked the chain from the post and tugged it. "Let's go. It's almost time for the show to start."

"Don't do this. My child is innocent."

"Your child means nothing to me. Although I imagine killing it will hurt your father. And to think it's all because you came for a visit. We thought he'd put you in hiding after Gerry went to your house."

"You sent that man?"

"So you did meet him. I had to wonder since he disappeared after that night. Dead, I assume?"

"He attacked me."

"As ordered. Your father needs to understand he messed with the wrong person. I worked too hard for a spot on the Cabal to give up now."

She frowned. She'd heard Ulric and Erryn speak of the Cabal. "You're part of the secret Lycan government?"

"Yes, but that would change if your father ever exposed me."

"Why not negotiate to make sure he doesn't?"

"Because I don't negotiate with humans. Now enough yapping. Let's go." The drag of the chain led her upstairs into a mudroom that led to a kitchen. There was also a door going outside.

Freedom!

Grabbing hold of the chain still around her neck, she tugged hard and unexpectedly. The man didn't teeter even a bit.

"Move!" he barked, giving it an even harder yank.

She stumbled after him. In her haste to cross the threshold of the front door, she missed the fact the ground dropped. Her foot hit hard enough to jolt right up her spine. She sucked in a breath and looked left then right. She recognized nothing. The cornfield to either side was not something in her parents' neighborhood or anywhere, for that matter, that she'd visited. In the driveway, two cars were parked. The men she'd met during her morning ride leaned against the vehicles, watching her.

Heads turned as lights bobbed in the distance, illuminating the winding dirt drive. She'd felt every bump coming in.

"We've got company," Smelly announced as if they hadn't all noticed.

Had Ulric come? He wouldn't know what he walked into.

Before she could breathe, he stepped from the car while Daddy emerged from the passenger side.

She whispered, "You came."

She'd have sworn she heard Ulric reply.

Always.

25

For a guy who'd promised to always protect Honey, Ulric had done a piss-poor job.

She had been kidnapped, and it had been a long, frustrating day of trying to track down who'd taken her. The blame of which resided on Ulric's shoulders. He should have been by her side.

It turned out the blame also partly belonged to Jacob because a ransom arrived demanding an exchange with Jacob. Said they would text the address an hour before the switch. An hour made a pretty wide circle to search, even with the help he'd called for. His Pack joined in the search, even as they had no clue what to even look for.

By the time they knew where to go, he'd managed to work himself into an almost berserker rage.

Honey was in danger. It had him seething with anger—and an impotence that didn't sit well.

And yet he insisted on driving when Jacob got the instructions. He ignored the "come alone" part. He and Jacob both knew they would have to act quickly and decisively if everyone was going to escape this alive.

They pulled into the driveway of a house literally planted in a corn field out in the middle of nowhere. Woods and marsh for hundreds of acres around.

He saw Honey right away, in her night clothes, swaying on her feet, the chain around her neck an affront to his senses.

The moment he emerged from the car, his gaze zeroed in on her, met and held hers. He tried to convey a promise. She would walk away from his.

He'd give his life to ensure it. It was almost moonrise, and he could feel the urge pulsing against his skin.

Would Honey know to use the element of surprise to move away from the man holding her chain?

Jacob started the talking first. "I should have outed you the first time I saw you stealing from the pool, Viper."

"And yet you didn't."

Jacob shrugged. "I saw no harm in a little skimming. Knew it would be a good bargaining chip for later. Only you had to go and start doing even worse things."

"You should have minded your business."

"You should have not gotten so greedy."

Ulric strode forward. "Let her go."

"The terms of the agreement were that Jacob come

alone in exchange for his daughter. It is now null and void." A smug reply.

Ulric clenched his fists as he stepped closer. "Whatever your problem, she has nothing to do with it. She's pregnant and needs special care, or she'll lose this baby."

"I'm a believer in survival of the fittest."

Ulric was close enough to smell the man. To smell...

"You're Lycan," he said almost accusingly.

Viper's eyes flashed. "And so are you. Who sent you against me?"

"No one. I'm here for Honey."

Viper wound the chain around her tighter on his fist, reeling her close. "Given all the interest in her, I have to wonder if maybe I shouldn't keep her. Although we'll have to do something about the welp in her belly."

Her eyes widened. "Ulric." The way she said it broke his heart.

Before he could reply, another car pulled into the drive and Silver emerged at a run, Quinn followed more calmly. She hollered, "Don't you dare harm her, Viper. You know the Cabal granted her leniency."

Viper glanced from Honey to Silver and back again before his smile turned grotesque. "Well, I'll be damned. This is the pregnant human you asked permission to study? Iris's daughter?" He laughed. "Isn't this a coincidence? The very woman I said should be killed for breaking our laws is also the daughter of my enemy."

It hit Ulric in that moment that Viper wasn't just Jacob's enemy, but Cabal. Several ranks above Ulric. But that didn't excuse his corruption.

"You said you'd trade." Jacob didn't manage his usual bluster.

"I lied. No one was ever walking away from tonight alive. But tell you what, I'll give the girl a running start." He dropped the chain and shoved Honey. "Go away. I'll deal with you later."

She backed away while coiling the length of chain.

"I said go!"

The yell galvanized her. She ran, right into the cornfield as twilight darkened. The moon brightened, and Ulric felt the urge to flip out.

But did he need to? He didn't smell a gun on Viper, and his posse seemed happy to just casually watch.

Not so Jacob, who pulled out a gun. "Stupid fucker. You just gave away your only advantage."

"Did I?" Viper grinned, not discomfited one bit.

Jakob took aim and drawled, "You might be new to the Cabal but surely you've heard the rumors."

"That you're a crack shot? Yes. But even you have limits." Viper's smile never wavered, which led to Ulric glancing around. Noting the three guys they'd seen upon arriving were taking off their shirts. More Lycans.

"Let me ask," Viper drawled, "do you want to die

quickly? Throat crushed maybe? Or slowly, where I eat you while you bleed out?"

"How did the Cabal ever make the mistake of accepting you as a member?" Because they were supposed to be the loftiest of them.

"That just shows why you're not if you can't see greatness," Viper hissed, and his teeth lengthened in his human face. He grew hair, but his body didn't contort.

"What the fuck?" exclaimed Jacob.

What the fuck indeed, given Viper didn't change like any Lycan Ulric knew.

He remained upright for one. His face furred and bulged slightly but didn't elongate into a muzzle. His fingers were clipped in hairy knuckles and claws. His jaw hinged even more to accommodate the slavering teeth. His eyes glowed an eerie yellow green.

But shit-your-pants scariest of all?

He talked in a grumbly, growly voice. "After I kill you, I'm going to find your mate and fuck her until that baby comes out."

Ulric charged, yelling in rage, blind with it. He slammed into the wolfman, and his fists started pounding.

Wham.

Wham.

Wham.

Kept hitting until he heard a strange noise coming from Viper.

He paused to find the fucker laughing. "What's so fucking funny?"

"You, thinking you can win. While you were beating me, they went after your woman."

He glanced at the cornfield, its stalks swaying in the moonlight.

There was a howl. Just one, but it sent a chill.

Before he could even think of running to her rescue, the shooting started.

26

ANY ELATION HONEY had felt seeing Ulric and her father coming to her rescue evaporated the moment she was told to run.

Everyone knew to stay out of the cornfields. Name one horror movie where that spooky-ass place actually sheltered anyone.

It didn't exist! Yet she had no other choice. She bolted for the rustling field of maize, expecting at any moment to be grabbed. A mouse scurrying to escape the hawk.

Despite knowing it was a supremely bad idea, she entered the dry stalks and pushed through them, making a godawful racket. Even slowing down didn't help much. She panted as she sought to see in the deepening gloom as twilight gave way to night.

A night that prickled the skin.

Oh no.

A glance overhead showed the full moon big and bright. Terrifying too. She'd planned to be back at their place before it happened or, if at her parents', to barricade herself in the theatre room and cry if anyone tried to get her out unless they got her a specific brand of ice cream she used to eat as a kid.

But instead of being somewhere safe, she was out in a fucking cornfield with nowhere to hide.

Which, of course, happened to be the moment she heard the first howl.

As if in reaction, she cramped. An excruciating clench of her belly bent her over with a gasp.

It eased, and she straightened. Maybe just one of those weird pregnancy things. She'd taken a step when the howl came again, only this time a second and third wolf joined the ululating.

A shudder went through her. Her skin continued to tingle, and all the hairs on her body lifted. Her stomach tightened with another contraction.

No. It was too soon. Damned moon. She needed cover. She'd find none out practically in the open, but the house offered no shelter either, not with that man calling himself Viper.

Had Ulric kicked his ass yet?

Ulric would know where to hide her. She flipped around and took the path back to the house. In her ragged haste, she practically ran into a wolf, and she couldn't have said who was more surprised.

It barked as she lunged, fingers reaching, scrabbling

for purchase, and somehow hitting an eye. She didn't gag when it popped like a grape under the pressure of her thumb.

The yelping wolf had no interest in further engaging, and she stumbled past.

Bang. Bang. The distant firing of a gun came with a sharp yelp. Had to be her dad fighting.

It also meant stray bullets. Best she not get too close, lest she find one by accident.

She sat on the ground, hugging her belly, grunting as another spasm zinged through her.

"It's too soon, peanut," she whispered. She clutched her belly and hunkered low against some flopping cornstalks, trying to push herself into a pocket of darkness away from the moon's rays.

The gunfire tapered off. The yelling came sporadic and indistinct. She closed her eyes and hugged her knees to her chest under her T-shirt, tucking her toes under the hem then pressing her face to her knees, her hair helping to cover flesh. Her hands squeezed in there. She did what she could to minimize her exposure to the light beaming down from the night sky.

Didn't make a difference. Her body felt it striking her scalp, penetrating the thin fabric of her clothes. The baby kicked and squirmed, lunging and spinning. She probably imagined she felt it chewing.

She knew puppies weren't born with dangerous teeth and claws. The ultrasound showed a baby.

What would it show now? Was peanut now a pea-wolf?

Not yet, she'd wager, because she still lived. She had to get to shelter.

A rustle lifted her head.

The snarl chilled her blood.

She saw the glow of its eyes first. A wolf stalking between the cornstalks, intent on her.

She rose to her feet, wavering as the waves of nausea and pain consumed her, blurring her vision, making her taste bile. She could smell death's fetid breath. The wolf slavered, the line of hanging drool repugnant.

When the wolf leaped, she didn't hold up her arms or run. She lunged and snarled right back, swiping with her hand. Tearing a stripe as she struck a blow to its muzzle. The wolf landed and skidded into some stalks before shaking its head.

It dared to lift its lip at her. She bared her own teeth as she attacked. Wildly. Without conscious thought to what she even did. Other than a need to strike.

Fight.

Live.

She won and staggered to her feet, uttering an eerie sound. She loped through the stalks, heading for the house. Emerging from the field to light and chaos. Bodies too.

Not all of them lying on the ground.

Ulric grappled with a monster. Her daddy shot a wolf. A car pulled in, and more people arrived to join the chaos.

Meanwhile Honey couldn't stay upright in all that moonlight. She collapsed to her knees whispering, "I don't feel good." She hit the ground on her ass then flopped to her back. She eyed her rippling belly and had time to think, "My parents should have called me Ripley," before passing out.

27

Ulric need to end this fight. Needed to help his mate, who writhed on the ground. But what the wolfman lacked in size he made up for in extras like those claws and strength.

Grappling took all Ulric's concentration, and yet when Jacob yelled, "Honey!" his head turned.

Wham.

The blow made him see stars. He might have lost his throat next if not for the bullet that hit the monster in the head, fired by none other than Quinn.

Silver hollered, "I told you we were supposed to take him in alive so he could stand trial."

"Waste of time and resources. Lycan law has only one sentence for traitors." Quinn didn't look apologetic as Ulric released the limp body.

"Honey." He whispered her name as he ran, sliding to his knees. Jacob held her head cradled in his lap.

"Something's wrong," the other man murmured. "She won't wake up."

Her body shuddered, her stomach rippling.

"We have to get her inside out of the moonlight." Ulric gritted his teeth against the wildness surging within. Before Jacob could struggle out from under Honey, Ulric scooped her up and ran for the house, only too late realizing it might have company.

When he paused in the doorway, Quinn urged him onward. "I've got your back, brother."

He followed her scent trail, wagering they'd kept her somewhere very secure—likely with few or no windows. The basement he found proved to be a perfect hideout from the moon, only Honey kept shivering.

He kept her in his arms as he stood helpless.

Silver clattered down the stairs. "I need you to hold her tight while I give her a shot."

"A shot of what?" he asked.

"Something to calm the baby."

He wanted to ask more questions, but the way Honey hung limp while her belly jiggled...

"Do it."

In the distance he heard more gunshots. Jacob didn't surprise him, but Quinn? Since when did he run around with a weapon?

The needle went in, and the doctor pushed the plunger. But she wasn't done with one. "You'll really have to hold on. This next one might get ugly."

He didn't know what she meant until Honey began thrashing. Her head snapped back, and her whole body went into convulsions. He almost lost his grip. As he readjusted, her face slammed forward, and she bit him right on the pec.

Bit him right through flesh, and he started bleeding.

She growled and hung on as her body quivered then calmed.

"One last one to help her sleep," the doctor said. The third needle didn't even make Honey flinch.

She collapsed against him, sound asleep, and yet he couldn't let her go. He held on to her as Jacob and Quinn brought down a mattress with blankets. Food and water as well.

When the old man would have stayed with them, it was Silver who dragged him away saying, "Go home to your wife. Let her know Honey's okay."

Apparently, Daisy hadn't been happy about being left behind. Even less happy that Silver had left Terror the kitten with her.

"Not before you answer some questions."

Silver shook her head. "You know the Cabal rules."

That thinned his lips. "Oh I do, and I will be having a chat with them. My family should have been off-limits." Jacob departed but not willingly or happy about it.

The Pack arrived in time to help with cleanup. AKA disposing of the bodies.

They thoroughly burned Viper. Dead wolves weren't a problem. Even dead men could be explained. But a cross between the two would have raised uncomfortable scrutiny. Bad enough Jacob knew and quite possibly his wife. At the same time, Ulric had to assume the Cabal trusted him, given the man knew all their financial secrets.

Would it be enough?

Hell, Ulric should be more worried about himself.

A Cabal member had died this night. There would be repercussions. But he'd do it all again to see Honey open her eyes the next morning and smile. "Morning, my Viking."

"Hey, Bee. How you feeling?"

"Hungry."

Which led to them demolishing the scant food in the kitchen. But she needed more. So they bundled her into a car and took her home, where her mother took one look and said, "Let me make you some pancakes." And bacon. And some potato thing that almost made him ask Daisy to marry him.

But surely Honey would know the recipe. And he was so damned happy she was okay that he treated her like glass that entire day.

It wasn't until that evening—right after dinner actually—that they finally sat down with her parents, and Silver, for a chat.

Honey eyed her dad and said, "I can't believe you work for the werewolf mob."

With that as an ice breaker, some details emerged to fill in the gaps of their knowledge such as how Jacob had been the Cabal accountant for decades with enough dirt to ensure his safety and that of his family.

"That didn't stop Viper from coming after you," was Ulric's reply.

To which Jacob pursed his lips. "Because he was a crooked fucker from the get-go and thought he could intimidate me into silence."

Silver then jumped in to explain Viper was a newer Cabal member, nominated at the unexpected death of another and not without argument. "There are some that considered him too hot-headed for the job."

"And crooked," Jacob added. "At first, I tried guiding him in the right direction, but he just wouldn't see reason. Since I didn't want him jeopardizing the entire operation, I reported him to the Cabal, which is when he threatened me and went after Honey thinking he could blackmail me by harming her."

"I don't understand, though," Ulric interrupted. "That was more than a month ago. How was it the Cabal hadn't already handled him?"

Silver had the answer. "He went into hiding."

Honey had a question for the doctor. "You knew all this and didn't tell us?"

The other woman shrugged. "Wasn't my place. My only concern is you and the baby."

The conversation could have gone on for hours after that, but Honey had enough. "I'm tired, and so is baby." She rose from the couch and grabbed Ulric's hand, as she did, saying, "We're going to bed."

When her mom opened her mouth—

Honey cut her off. "My fiancé is coming with me, or we're going to a hotel."

Which led to Jacob saying, "We need a walk. Now."

Ulric could have told him not to bother, as he had no intention of having sex. He didn't need a medical degree to know she'd almost died.

Only Honey apparently didn't realize it. The moment they got to her bedroom she was kissing him.

"We shouldn't. You need to rest."

"What I need is you inside me. Right now."

"But—"

"Less talk. More touching," she whispered against his lips before kissing him.

It was hard to say no. So he didn't. He just made sure he did the bulk of the work. Kissing every inch of her as if reassuring himself she was uninjured. Playing with her breasts and nipples until she arched from the bed and panted, begging.

Before he gave her what she wanted, he slid between her legs for a taste, plying her clit with his tongue, spreading her nether lips for a lick. Only when she had her first little orgasm did he relent and slide up her body, giving himself the leverage needed to nudge her sex with his cock.

She didn't want his gentle pressure. Her legs

locked around his hips and dragged him close, sheathing him tightly. He groaned as he held taut inside her.

She writhed. Wiggled. Shimmied.

He couldn't help but follow her demanding lead. Grinding and thrusting. Pushing deep until her channel did that clench thing that happened when he hit the right spot.

He kept thrusting. His gaze on her face. When her eyes opened and their gazes locked, he mouthed, *I love you.*

"You're mine," she said.

The magical words to make him come.

And they kept him a grinning man even as he spent the next three days being tortured by his new mother-in-law, who did indeed manage to throw a wedding before the baby was born.

His in-laws didn't seem too perturbed at getting a werewolf as a son-in-law, although Jacob did pull him aside to show him a silver bullet and mutter, "Hurt her and you'll be eating this."

As if he'd ever harm his mate.

The wedding happened as planned. He couldn't have said what they ate, or said, or even what they danced to. The only thing he would always remember was his glowing bride when she looked him dead in the eye and, when it came time to say "I do," chose to grin and instead howled, "I yabba dabba do!"

EPILOGUE

The month after the wedding passed much too quickly. While they could have stayed at Honey's place, instead they went back to the house in the woods with all its equipment.

The bigger Honey's belly grew, the more Ulric panicked. Not that he let it show. Honey glowed and had no fear at all. She kept telling him everything was going to be fine.

Meanwhile he wanted to know what these so-called vitamin shots of Dr. Silver's contained. At the same time, it didn't matter if it kept Honey alive.

On the subject of Dr. Silver, he'd never gotten to discover more about her involvement with the Cabal other than she worked directly for them. Answered only to them. And hadn't been involved in the Viper thing at all. Or so she claimed.

Honey trusted her, and Ulric knew they needed

her, so he let it go. Poking it would only unleash unpleasant consequences—for him.

As the full moon approached, the itch hit him harder than usual. Having not shifted the last time left him full of tension.

The day of the full orb, Honey and the doctor took no chances, locking themselves downstairs. Honey went to sleep early by design, and he went for a short four-legged run.

It was two days later that the contractions started.

There was much screaming and cursing. By Dr. Silver, who told Ulric to get out of her way if he was going to keep almost fainting every time she checked Honey's cervix.

Eventually the moment came. Honey gripped his hand tight as he stood to the side and watched a head appear then shoulders, arms, legs.

In a gush of fluid that made him queasy slipped a slippery body, leading him to exclaim, "Holy fuck, a baby."

"No shit. Hopefully your son gets his mother's brains," Dr. Silver said dryly as she knotted the cord and flipped the baby for a smack on the back.

It took a second before the baby gasped and yelled.

His son's first cry.

I have a son.

Ulric almost fell over again, probably why Dr. Silver muttered, "Out of the way. Take this." The baby got practically tossed at Ulric, who held him still as a bomb.

As Silver knelt, he noticed the abnormal amount of blood still flowing. A glance at Honey showed her smile fading as her eyes fluttered.

"What's happening?"

Rather than reply, Silver yanked on the cord and out came a hunk of—

He turned and heaved, the baby tucked to his chest. "What was that?" he finally said when he got his gagging under control.

"Let's just say your wife didn't escape this pregnancy entirely unscathed."

He whirled. "Is she okay?"

Silver nodded. "She should be, but she won't ever have another child."

His head bowed as he inwardly whispered, *I'm sorry*. Then, "Does she know?"

The doctor nodded. "She was always aware this might happen." And she still chose to go through with it was the unspoken part.

"Where's the baby?" Honey's faint request drew him to her side. He leaned down and gently placed the bundled baby in his wife's arms.

It led to a sudden squalling. Honey beamed at their squishy red-faced son and declared, "He's perfect."

Even Terror agreed. The kitten took to sleeping in the crib with Michael—named after Michael J. Fox for his iconic role in *Teen Wolf*—and hissing at anyone who got too close other than Mom and Dad.

A perfect family for a werewolf.

A happily ever after at last for Ulric.

Dr. Erryn Silver presented her findings to the Cabal virtually.

"The pregnancy was successful."

"Only because of your intervention," argued one of the members.

"The treatment protocol has flaws," another pointed out. "The mother reacted to the moonlight and would have died if not for Silver."

"But she proved it's possible," said yet another via the anonymous group call.

"One successful birth doesn't mean it will work for everyone." But it was a start that Erryn hoped to build on.

"The child is human, correct?" asked the deepest of the voices.

"All tests show negative for the Lycan markers." For now. Erryn intended to keep an eye on the baby because the fact Honey reacted so violently to the moon had to mean something.

"Meaning the Lycanthropy was not passed on despite the child being male."

"Maybe. It might be years before we know for sure.

I recommend monitoring on the full moons until the child reaches adulthood."

"Obviously." Then after a pause. "Was there something else you wanted?"

An apology for not listening to her about getting rid of the Viper cancer in the Cabal midst would have been nice, but she knew better than to expect accolades from this group. Instead, she asked for something they could give. "I want the funding and permission to seek out other possible live births."

Her demand was met with laughter. "You think there are rogue Lycans roaming the world?"

While some mocked, a raspy voice, however, said, "Let's say you're correct. How would you find them?"

"From my research, I've isolated a few genetic markers that might be pointers. Running them against databases from the around the world I've made some hits." The ancestry DNA kits provided a treasure trove once their databases were hacked.

"You've contacted outsiders?" a huffed accusation.

"Never, but with your permission, I'd like to observe some of the people flagged to see if I'm correct."

"Very well. But not alone."

She frowned. "I don't need help."

"Given the information you have, and the danger you might encounter, this isn't an option. We'll send a Cabal operative to join you."

It shouldn't have surprised her when she got a call

from the very annoying Quinn, who sounded amused as he said, "Hey, Doc. I hear you need a bodyguard."

ARE YOU READY TO GO ON A WILD ADVENTURE IN *WEREWOLF BODYGUARD*?

For more books and fun see EveLanglais.com

Ingram Content Group UK Ltd.
Milton Keynes UK
UKHW040644070623
423021UK00004B/73